SCREWING
SINATRA

SCREWING SINATRA

P MOSS

@IDWPUBLISHING
IDWPUBLISHING.COM

979-8-88724-356-6
28 27 26 25   1 2 3 4

EDITOR FOR SQUIDHAT PRESS:
Scott Dickensheets

EDITOR FOR IDW:
Alonzo Simon

AUTHOR PHOTO:
Ginger Bruner

COVER & DESIGN:
Brian Kolek

The IDW logo is registered in the U.S. Patent and Trademark Office. IDW Publishing, a division of Idea and Design Works, LLC. Editorial offices: 14144 Ventura Blvd, Suite 210, Sherman Oaks, CA 91423. IDW Publishing does not read or accept unsolicited submissions of ideas, stories, or artwork. Printed in Canada.

Davidi Jonas, CEO
Andrew DeBaker, CFO
Gregg Katz, General Counsel
Tara McCrillis, President Publishing Operations
Bobby Curnow, Editor in Chief
Aub Driver, VP Marketing
Gregg Katzman, Sr. Manager Public Relations
Warren Buchanan, Licensing Manager
Lauren LePera, Sr. Managing Editor
Shauna Monteforte, Sr. Director of Manufacturing Operations
Jamie Miller, Director Publishing Operations
Jasmine Gonzalez, Director Ecommerce Operations
Alison Quin, Sr. Director IT
Ryan Balkam, Specialty Market Sales Manager
Nathan Widick, Director of Design
Neil Uyetake, Sr. Art Director, Design & Production

Ted Adams and Robbie Robbins, IDW Founders

EU RP (for authorities only)
eucomply OÜ
Pärnu mnt. 139b – 14
11317 Tallinn, Estonia
hello@eucompliancepartner.com
+33757690241

Contracting Partner: Tara McCrillis, IDW Publishing | EU RP Partner: Marko Novkovic, CEO *for the gentlemen*

Although based upon actual events
that changed America forever,
this book is a work of fiction

CHAPTER 1

March 1960

Looking exquisite in a canary-yellow Oleg Cassini cocktail dress accented with a double strand of perfectly matched pearls, Jacqueline Kennedy walked down the second-floor corridor of the Sands Hotel, excited to surprise her husband, who was in Las Vegas taking a break from campaigning before the New Hampshire presidential primary. She knocked on the door and heard his muffled voice tell someone it was probably room service with the champagne, then pushed her way inside as John Kennedy opened up wearing only his boxer shorts while Marilyn Monroe sat on the edge of the bed wearing nothing at all.

"Jackie, I can explain," he stammered. "It's not what you think."

"What is it, then?"

Again, the stammer.

"Do you think I've been blind all these years, Jack? It used to be low-hanging fruit like maids and cocktail waitresses, but ever since you've been hobnobbing with Sinatra and that Rat Pack of his, you've stepped up in class."

"You think I have class?" Marilyn cooed in a wispy voice. "What a sweet thing to say."

"Dammit, Marilyn," John Kennedy snapped. "Will you get the hell out of here!"

Jackie sized up the blond bombshell. But instead of seeing the movie star most men dreamed of having their way with, she saw the eyes of a woman who, even with all the adulation, seemed lonely and empty inside.

"Hopefully one day you will meet a man who can see past the obvious," Jackie said as she sat beside Marilyn on the bed, then tickled her fingers across the naked woman's cheek. "But in the meantime, don't you think you deserve to have sex with a Kennedy who can last longer than two minutes?"

"Stop it, Jackie."

"I studied a lot more than art history during my year in Paris," said Mrs. Kennedy, grinning at her husband as she brushed her lips against Marilyn's.

Any other woman and Jack Kennedy's dick would have been throbbing, but this was his *wife*. The mother of his daughter, and she knew it tortured him to watch as she kissed Marilyn's neck and her shoulders as the movie star's nipples stiffened at the warm breath on her skin.

"Dammit, Jackie. I demand you stop this *right now!*"

"Shut up and watch, Jack." Mrs. Kennedy slipped out of her clothes, naked except for the double strand of perfectly matched pearls, then eased Marilyn back on the bed. "Hopefully you'll learn something."

CHAPTER 2

The audience hung on every note as Frank Sinatra commanded the sold-out Copa Room at the Sands, belting out the final verse of "The Lady Is a Tramp" only to be disrupted by laughter as a boozed-up Dean Martin carried Sammy Davis Jr. onto the stage.

"I'd like to thank the NAACP for this award," Dean slurred, stumbling over the words as he put down the pint-sized song-and-dance man, then grabbed a bottle from the drinks cart that was front and center at every show.

"Dammit, Dean," scolded Sinatra. "We need to talk about your drinking."

"What happened? Did I miss a round?"

And so it went. The Rat Pack Summit. Fractured songs and nonstop shtick as Dean—the greatest straight man in showbiz during his years setting up punch lines for Jerry Lewis—was now the one delivering quick-witted comebacks while aloof comic Joey Bishop was the glue that held it all together. It was a show born out of a serious concert format until Frank caught wild trumpet man Louis Prima's act at the Desert Inn. He had marveled at the enthusiastic audience reaction to all the looseness and fun, and he decided to scrap the structure and make every Rat Pack show a party.

Hair beginning to thin as he crept into middle age, Sinatra still looked like a million in his Sy Devore tuxedo as he noticed a cute 13-year-old girl sitting with her parents and asked her to stand up. "What's your name, doll?"

"Gladys," she said with a big smile, basking in the spotlight. "Gladys Anderson, and I'm going to be a showgirl when I grow up."

"I bet you'll be a knockout," Sinatra told her, leading the audience in a round of applause. "And there is someone else here tonight who you are all going to want to applaud. More than applaud, you're going to vote for him."

A spotlight hit the man seated ringside with casino boss Jack Entratter.

"The right man to lead us into the new decade, into a future of limitless possibility: the honorable senator from Massachusetts and the next president of the United States, John Fitzgerald Kennedy!"

As Kennedy took a bow, Dean joked to Sinatra. "What did you say his name was?"

After the final encore, Frank's dressing room was where they usually would unwind before invading the casino to kick-start a late night of drunken debauchery. Sammy, who Frank had nicknamed Smokey, not because of his dark skin but because he inhaled four packs a day, was there with May Britt, the Swedish stunner who had just wrapped a star turn in the gangster flick *Murder, Inc*. British actor Peter Lawford, who Frank had for no apparent reason nicknamed Charlie, the fifth onstage member of the Rat Pack and often the target of Sinatra's practical jokes, straightened his tie in the mirror. He was good-looking and admitted it, but his talent was an octave below his ambition.

Married to Kennedy's sister Pat, Lawford had introduced Frank to Jack a few years earlier, and the two of them—through the common bond of chasing pussy—had become fast friends. And it was Pat who had put up $10,000 to option the story of a group of ex-army buddies who heist five Vegas casinos that would become the movie *Ocean's 11*. It was a project Lawford had hoped would be a starring vehicle for himself, an idea that Warner Brothers quickly shit-canned as the studio instead considered top stars William Holden and Jack Lemmon, unaware that Sinatra had plans to make it into a Rat Pack home movie. And when Frank Sinatra wanted something, he usually got it, turning the serious caper script into a camped-up musical comedy that the Rat Pack shot during the day before returning to the Copa Room to start the merry-go-round all over again.

"Time for me to cut out, pally," Dean told Frank as he finished his drink. "Got an early call in the morning."

"We don't have to be on the set until after lunch. Have another drink."

Frank and Dean didn't hang out all that often, as by the time Sinatra got rolling, Dean was heading upstairs to hit the sack. Dean loved the booze and the broads, but his real passion was golf, and he had an 8:00 a.m. tee time.

As Sinatra poured himself another drink, Jack Kennedy walked in with his wife.

"Mrs. Kennedy, what a pleasant surprise."

"Cut the crap, Frank," she told the man she viewed as nothing more than her husband's pimp. "I've had enough surprises from you tonight."

"We're on our way to a late supper," said Jack, tall and charismatic with a square jaw and impressive head of hair. "Just wanted to stop by and say that I enjoyed the show and to thank you for introducing me to the audience. Hopefully I picked up a few votes."

"Anything to help you get elected, Jack. Even if it's one vote at a time."

"You mean one blonde at a time, don't you, Frank?" Jackie snapped as she took her husband's arm and walked out the door of the dressing room and into the casino.

"For God sake, Jackie. Would it have hurt you to be civil to the man? Having my name linked with his is going to get me elected."

"That greaseball couldn't get you elected dog catcher. He comes from nothing. No breeding and no class," she said, walking and talking with her usual measured rhythm. She stopped and looked her husband dead in the eye. "If you hope to have any chance of moving into the White House, you're going to need me to charm the housewives of America with a look inside what the magazines tell them is a modern-day Camelot. But don't forget that I can just as easily see to it that you lose."

"Don't threaten me, Jackie."

"I have had more than my share of private disgrace, but you will *not* humiliate me in front of the entire country." She backed her husband against a slot machine and again looked him dead in the eye. "So, if you want to be elected president, keep your dick in your pants. Because if I ever catch you with Marilyn again, or if you publicly embarrass me in any way, I swear to God I will castrate you."

CHAPTER 3

Sinatra thrived on the nonstop action of Las Vegas, but after a three-week run at the Sands, he was happy to be back home in Palm Springs. Though no matter where he hung his hat, his world never stopped spinning.

"Make sure the hospital bill is paid and that there is some cash in his pocket when they send him home," he told his attorney, Mickey Rudin.

"Consider it done."

"Anonymously."

"Of course."

An oversized ashtray on the low glass coffee table in the living room was slightly out of place but not for long, as Sinatra was a perfectionist. There was a place for everything and everything in its place at his two-and-a-half-acre estate on Wonder Palms Road, which overlooked the seventeenth fairway of the Tamarisk Country Club. Floor-to-ceiling windows faced the pool, and the house was filled with modern orange furniture, as that was his favorite color. His Best Supporting Actor Oscar for *From Here to Eternity* sat on a lighted shelf visible from anywhere in the living room.

Since planting his flag in Palm Springs, California, Sinatra had been embraced by the close-knit desert community and felt a responsibility to continually repay that kindness. Whether it was spearheading the fund drive for a new school or coming to the aid of a stranger who was up against it, no cause was too big or too small. But his gravel-voiced attorney in the blue pinstripe suit had made the three-hour drive from his Beverly Hills office primarily to discuss settlement of a lawsuit brought by an annoying drunk Sinatra had slugged at a Hollywood nightclub for making lewd remarks about his date.

"The jerk was way out of line, Mickey. I'm not paying to settle his bullshit lawsuit."

"You have a history, Frank."

Sinatra was five foot seven and skinny as a rake, but that had never stopped him from punching out someone twice his size. He flicked his lighter and fired up a Chesterfield, his cigarette of choice since the tobacco company started writing big checks for him to sponsor their product.

"If we take this to court, you'll lose," the attorney said.

"Not a fucking penny."

"Did you hit him?"

"Of course I fucking hit him."

"Say that in front of a jury and you'll end up paying five times as much as we can settle for now." Mickey took a sip of iced tea. "That temper of yours is going to be the end of you one day, Frank. You probably can't even remember how many photographers you slugged for harassing Ava."

Plenty, Sinatra remembered, as he and ex-wife number two had been tabloid fodder for years.

"Sometimes you have to realize you can't win the fight and move on."

"Not a fucking penny."

"Let it go, Frank. Settle the suit and enjoy a few days relaxing here at home."

And what a home it was with vaulted ceilings, formal dining room, several guest suites, and a fully equipped darkroom to accommodate the master's hobby as an amateur shutterbug. Tennis court and a pool heated for late-night frolic. It even had a separate building he called the funhouse, where he pursued his passion for model railroading with an elaborate setup that could run six trains at once, one of them passing through a miniature replica of his hometown, Hoboken, New Jersey.

Sinatra considered Mickey Rudin the smartest man he knew, and his lawyer had rewarded that trust over the years by protecting his interests and steering him away from deals that seemed too good to be true. So, he agreed to settle the suit but never took his foot off the gas. For Frank Sinatra, life was a nonstop party of booze and broads. He was the king of midnight but also worked tirelessly. *Ocean's 11* had wrapped, and two more film projects were on tap. Constantly recording, he released albums on his Reprise label, as well as cranking out long players by a roster of other radio mainstays. Plus, new Rat Pack shows were booked at the Sands through the end of the year.

"Stick around, Mickey. I'm having a few people over tonight."

"Next time, Frank. I've got to get back for dinner with a new client."

"Cancel it."

"It's important."

"That cute trick from Vegas you like will be here."

Mickey Rudin smiled. "I guess the dinner isn't that important."

CHAPTER 4

Jimmy Van Heusen was a three-time Academy Award–winning composer, but his real talent was wrangling beautiful women. Whether they be Hollywood starlets or working girls from Vegas, the party never really got started until Jimmy showed up. Like flipping a switch, a casual evening with a few friends would morph into a wingding with champagne and Nat King Cole on the reel-to-reel the second he walked through the door with the female party favors.

Sinatra was a wine-and-dine romantic but often wanted it quick and easy, valuing the fair exchange provided by hookers since he did not have to deal with them emotionally. Cash as quid pro quo for a few laughs and some sport fucking. Still, he treated hookers like ladies, lighting cigarettes and topping off their champagne, often saying that he preferred an honest working girl to a conniving starlet. Looking upon sex as more than just a physical pleasure, he was positive it made him sing better, made him looser and more confident. And when Jimmy, his neighbor and pal, showed up with a half dozen stunners from Vegas, he was raring to go.

Frank's valet, George Jacobs, kept glasses full as the men joked, the women dazzled, and Mickey Rudin quickly disappeared to one of the guest bedrooms with the cute little trick he had blown off his client dinner for. But the guest of honor was a fish out of water. A 70-year-old fossil wearing a conservative suit and tie with round-rimmed glasses and hair you could count. A man who, even in the middle of a booze and broads free-for-all, Frank addressed with respect as Mr. Ambassador.

Joe Kennedy was Boston Irish, Harvard educated and had married the mayor's daughter. He had taken aim at a career in banking but veered quickly toward the wrong side of the law, enticed by the lure of the big money to be made as a bootlegger during Prohibition. Smuggling illegal alcohol earned him the bankroll he used, with the aid of inside information, to short sell stocks and amass a fortune during the 1929 Wall Street crash that brought on the Great Depression—money he used in 1938 to buy himself the U.S. ambassadorship to the United Kingdom. He had set his sights on the presidency, but it was a political career cut short when he went on record as saying that Hitler was just a blowhard and not a threat to anyone. So, twenty years later, he set his sights on buying the White House for his son.

George served Joe Kennedy a highball. The valet was likable, in his mid-thirties with an easy smile. But the ambassador looked at him with disgust.

"Is there something wrong with your drink, sir?"

"For god sake, Francis," Kennedy grumbled. "Can't you get any white help?"

Sinatra and his trusted valet both let the insult slide, knowing that the Kennedy patriarch had invited himself to be Frank's houseguest for a reason, something important. So, Frank kept the conversation light as he sipped his usual Jack Daniel's over ice and waited to find out what it was. He lit the ambassador's cigar and asked which of the girls he fancied.

"One is as good as another," said Kennedy, who had a reputation for treating hookers like shit, as did his son-in-law Peter Lawford, who got his kicks beating up black streetwalkers. "Just make sure there is a whore in my room when I retire for the night."

Which, for the old man, was soon. He made quick work of the hooker, then snored through the merriment of a wingding that carried on into the wee hours.

Bright sunlight beamed through the windows as Sinatra welcomed the new day, finding his houseguest waiting impatiently in the living room wearing a starched collar and dark three-piece suit.

"Good morning, Mr. Ambassador," Frank greeted him with a cheery smile. He was wearing a colorful sport shirt and slacks as he made himself comfortable on a sleek chair across from his guest. "Would you like some breakfast?"

"It's almost noon, for God sake."

George set a tray of coffee and pastries on the table between them and asked if they wanted anything else.

"Maybe Sambo has some dishes to do," Kennedy said, motioning to George.

Apologetically, Frank told George to please give them some privacy. Then he made small talk, but the old man was having none of it and got straight to the point.

"America is not ready to put a Catholic in the White House, and Jack needs your help."

"I've been committed to Jack's candidacy since the beginning."

"He isn't focused. Before the New Hampshire primary, instead of shaking hands with voters, Jack was cavorting with you and your Rat Pack at the Sands."

"And he won by a landslide," Frank said, taking a sip of his coffee, then lighting a Chesterfield.

"You are deliberately missing the point, which is that you are an enabler," the old man complained. "My son is a war hero, handsome, with a *Life* magazine cover family. But it pains me to say that Jack would rather chase women with you than become president of the United States."

Frank wanted to smile but thought better of it.

"It will all be different when Bobby runs," Kennedy continued, thinking ahead.

"Bobby? He's still a kid."

"Thirty-five, and he's the one with the ambition. More importantly, the drive, as there is nothing he won't do to get what he wants, and he knows that it's never too early to start. He's already building his national profile by going after racketeers as lead attorney of the Senate McClellan Committee, making a name for himself by taking a hard stance against organized crime for when it's his turn to run."

"A Kennedy dynasty?"

"Jack, Bobby, then it will be Teddy's turn." The old man straightened his glasses precisely. "But before any of it can happen, Jack is going to need Sam Giancana's help in West Virginia."

"Bobby called Sam a giggly little girl at those nationally televised racket hearings, then triggered government surveillance that has made his life a living hell every day since. So, if you think the boss of the Outfit is going to help any Kennedy, you are out of your mind."

"Hubert Humphrey has a big lead in West Virginia, and we need union support to win the primary."

"Why would any union help Jack after Bobby tore Teamsters president Jimmy Hoffa a new asshole at the same hearings?"

"Forget the Teamsters. It's the United Mine Workers that we need. The Outfit controls that union and, with a little pressure, can flip their support our way."

"What's so important about a small state like West Virginia?"

"If Jack can prove to the Democratic Party power brokers that he can win in a heavily Protestant state, he will all but lock up the nomination. Then, in November, assuming things play out according to polling projections, to put Jack in the White House all Giancana will need to do is deliver Illinois. And since he already controls Chicago, that should be a certainty."

"The only certainty is that Sam won't help you."

"Allow me to remind you that I have known Sam Giancana since he was hijacking beer trucks in the twenties."

"A relationship that Bobby, serving as Jack's campaign manager, put the kibosh on, which is why you need to use me as a go-between. But I can tell you right now that he will tell you to piss in your hat."

"Giancana did not rise to become the top man in the Outfit by passing up golden opportunities."

"So far, this opportunity is sounding completely one-sided." Sinatra exhaled a stream of smoke, causing the old man to squint. "What's in it for Sam?"

"Once Jack is elected, all Senate and FBI inquiries into racketeering will stop, including all wiretap surveillance."

"No matter how far back you and Sam go, he will never trust any Kennedy after Bobby tried to make a monkey out of him on TV."

"I guarantee that Bobby will do his part to uphold the family's end of the bargain. I need you to tell Sam that he can trust the Kennedys because *I say* he can trust the Kennedys."

"You had better hope so, or he'll put a bullet between your eyes."

"During Prohibition, I witnessed Sam Giancana murder men for less, so rest assured that my sons will do exactly as I tell them."

"Why are you pushing so hard, Mr. Ambassador? Is it because you don't think that, as things stand, Jack can win the presidency?"

"Jack *is* going to win."

"Then why is fixing the election so important to you?"

"Call it insurance, Francis."

"Or is it that you don't want to sweat out an honest game when it's so much easier to deal from the bottom of the deck?"

CHAPTER 5

"What's good here?" Sinatra asked the man seated with him in the corner booth of a neighborhood spaghetti joint on the north side of Chicago.

"I wouldn't know," Giancana said.

"Then why did we make the drive?"

"Because since the McClellan hearings, the Feds have my phone tapped. All my broads' phones are tapped, and even the phones at restaurants where I usually eat are tapped. I carry a roll of dimes in my pocket because the only way I can talk to anybody is on a goddam payphone. That's why," complained Sam Giancana, a gruff-looking man in his fifties whose exquisitely tailored silk suit cost as much as a new Cadillac. The man collected antique silver tea services and Dresden figurines, but behind the refinement was a vicious killer responsible one way or another for over two hundred murders.

The conversation paused as Sam was served a glass of red wine and Sinatra his usual Jack Daniel's on the rocks. Then the most powerful gangster in America continued to grouse once the waiter was out of earshot.

"Who knows where else that weasel Bobby Kennedy has microphones planted," he complained, glancing at his bodyguard who kept an eye on things from a stool at the end of the bar. "And how many waiters and bartenders have been bribed to keep their eyes and ears open."

Gone was the pal quick with a laugh who enjoyed a good time. In his place, Sinatra saw a man imprisoned by paranoia and asked Giancana why he didn't just turn the tables on Bobby.

"I had Jimmy Hoffa bug his house and his office back when this bullshit first started, and all I found out was the punk is a big nothing. Almost never drinks, doesn't screw around on his wife or even swear. What kind of dirt can you dig up on a motherfucker who doesn't even *swear*? He's the most boring son of a bitch who ever drew breath." He looked around the restaurant. "Check out all the people staring at us from other tables."

"I'm famous," Sinatra said, lighting a cigarette.

"I'm not."

"Says the man whose name is in the newspaper more often than it isn't."

"How do we know the Feds didn't follow us here? That fag prick Hoover is providing all the FBI manpower the weasel asks for. Anything to fuck with the Outfit." Giancana lit a cigar and plugged it into the corner of his mouth. "This is a real problem, Frank. Not just for me but for all the bosses. A problem that makes it tough for any of us to do business."

"A problem I can fix."

"I love you like a brother, Frank," said the gangster, holding up his hand to show off a star sapphire pinky ring that had been a gift from Sinatra. "But if *we* can't fix this, you sure as fuck can't."

Sinatra loved gangsters. He loved their world and everything about them since 1942, when Willie Moretti jammed a gun in Tommy Dorsey's mouth to make him release Frank from his contract with the band. But as much as Giancana and some of the other high-profile Outfit guys allowed him to get close, it was never all the way. He was not one of them. But if he could play a key part in pulling off the biggest heist in American history, the White House, maybe he would be. He spelled out Joe Kennedy's offer.

"Why the fuck do you think we're eating here instead of the place that makes the best red sauce in Chicago? That old man's asshole son. That's why. The weasel who tried to crack me open on national television."

"Joe says he can control Bobby."

"That old man can't even control his bladder."

"He says that once Jack is in office, all government harassment will stop and you can go back to doing business as usual."

"He's a liar, Frank. And a coward who sent you because he's afraid to face me."

"The two of you go all the way back to Prohibition."

"He made a fortune bringing scotch over the water from Europe—good scotch nobody else could get because he had society connections through his wife's family, but he stayed clear of the action and was never within ten miles of a raid. Not once getting his hands dirty, and you can't trust a man who won't get his hands dirty."

As they ate manicotti that both agreed was not too bad, Sinatra changed the subject by opening his wallet and showing off recent snapshots of his kids. Giancana talked about a couple hot numbers he had lined up for them later, then threw out an idea he had been kicking around about opening a Vegas-style supper club and showroom outside Chicago city limits in unincorporated Cook County. A location far from the action that seemed, on the surface, to be a bad idea, but Giancana had a keen business sense, once prompting the compliment from Meyer Lansky that he was the only Italian who handled money like a Jew.

Then the gangster circled back.

"If Joe Kennedy really is on the square about stopping all the government harassment, it would be a huge win for the Outfit. How do you read the old man, Frank?"

"Getting Jack into the White House means more to him than anything else in this world."

Giancana took a sip of wine, then thought for a moment.

"Joe Kennedy knows he's a dead man if he crosses me. Which leads me to believe that, with so much at stake, maybe this time he *can* be trusted."

"Then I'll tell him it's a deal."

"Not so fast, Frank."

CHAPTER 6

"Joe Kennedy has always been a one-way asshole," yelled an angry voice at the back of the room, followed by another even louder. "No fucking way we do business with the Kennedys after that weasel Bobby attacked us at those Senate hearings."

"We need to put all that in the past," Giancana told a gathering of Outfit bosses, a cigar plugging the side of his mouth as he stood in front of a window in a corner suite at the Drake Hotel overlooking Lake Michigan.

"Are you fucking serious, Sam?" yelled Carlos Marcello, boss of New Orleans. "That punk called you a giggling little girl on television for the whole country to see."

"And when the time comes, he'll pay for it. But right now, what's more important is that we're fighting a losing battle." Giancana polished his watch with his handkerchief, allowing the point to sink in. "And if the Outfit is going to survive, we need to be smart and look to the future."

"Things were good before those fucking hearings," griped Santo Trafficante from Florida. "Now I can't even talk to my broad on the phone without some Fed pulling his pud while he listens in."

"That harassment is not going to stop until *we* do something to stop it," Giancana said. "And right now, I don't see any other way to take the heat off than to get in bed with the Kennedys."

Organized crime bosses from all over the map were not convinced, so Giancana kept pushing. "Bottom line is that if we get Jack Kennedy elected, he's agreed to stop coming after us."

"What about his weasel brother's investigation of the Teamsters?" demanded a voice from Detroit. "The unions are our bread and butter."

"I'll make it part of the deal that the Feds lay off Hoffa's Teamsters *and* all the other unions."

"What's to stop the Kennedys from welshing on the deal after we get Jack elected?" Trafficante demanded to know. "Dammit, Sam, you know those rat bastards can't be trusted."

"They cross us, and I'll drag every one of those Irish pricks down to the bayou and feed them to the gators," Marcello yelled.

"Why don't we just back Nixon?" Trafficante wanted to know. "He's been doing business with us for years. Got us some government contracts and doesn't try to screw the unions."

"But he hasn't done a goddam thing to stop the McClellan Committee or the wiretaps," Giancana pointed out.

"Because as vice president Nixon doesn't have a lot of power," Trafficante said. "But that will change once his ass is in the Oval Office."

"We don't know that for sure," Giancana roared back. "But with Kennedy, we have the old man's word that Jack will play ball."

"I'd feel a lot more comfortable if it was Jack's word," Trafficante said.

"At least we have a track record with Nixon. Backing him is the safe play."

"The Outfit did not grow to become bigger than General Motors by playing it safe!" Giancana yelled at the men in the room. "We use power to crush our enemies, and it's made every one of us rich. We've never backed down from a fight, and we're not going to fucking start now!"

The other bosses saw the logic in what he was saying, but several still balked at dealing with the Kennedys.

"I don't need your fucking approval to go ahead with this deal," Giancana told them, asserting his power. "I called you here because working in solidarity is what makes us strong, and it's important for the future of the Outfit that we are all in agreement. You guys need to see that when we get Jack elected, not only will the heat be off but he'll be in our pocket. We already own governors and congressmen; isn't it about time we owned a president?"

His point hit home, and the room quickly united.

"I'm glad you all agree." Giancana smiled, confirming his power over the other bosses. "I'm going to sit down with Joe Kennedy and make the deal."

Trafficante stood to emphasize a point. "Just make sure that cocksucker understands that nobody ever welshed on the Outfit and lived to tell about it."

CHAPTER 7

"What do colored people want, George?" Jack Kennedy asked as Sinatra's valet served him an icy daiquiri under an umbrella by the pool at Wonder Palms.

"What do *you* want, Senator?"

"It's Jack. Call me Jack."

"What do you want, Jack?"

"I want to fuck every girl in California." He smiled as, through the green lenses of his trademark tortoiseshell sunglasses, he checked out a couple of girls sunning on lounge chairs. Grateful that his wife hated Frank, preferring to remain at home with their young daughter, Caroline, which left him free to screw all the girls he wanted without having to sneak around.

"With a campaign platform like that, Senator, you can't lose."

"Jack, goddam it. Call me Jack or I'll send you back to Mississippi."

"I'm from Louisiana. In Mississippi, they eat Catholics, which means they hate you a lot worse than they hate me."

"What are you two kibitzing about?" Sinatra asked as he sat down.

"Discussing my campaign platform," said Jack as he lit an H. Upmann petit corona. "Right, George?"

"That's right, Senator."

"Jack, goddam it."

As George went about his business, Sinatra saw Jack ogling the girls.

"They're just decoration. The real talent will be here in a few minutes." Then Frank got serious. "And speaking of the campaign…"

"My father told me that you've come on board to help get out the primary vote."

"Did he tell you everything?"

"You can assure Sam Giancana that I will honor the deal." He gave his friend a pat on the back. "And I can't tell you how much I appreciate everything you're doing. With Humphrey polling well in the East, I need all the help I can get."

"I'm all in, Jack. And not just working the phones and calling in favors. I'm going out on the campaign trail to meet the voters face-to-face."

"Bobby and Dad think your image as a swinger will have a negative effect, but I think a healthy dose of Hollywood star power is just what my campaign needs." Jack thought ahead and smiled. "Once I'm in the White House, we can have orgies on Air Force One. I'll even make you ambassador to Lynchburg, Tennessee, where you can drink Jack Daniel's straight from the tap."

"Let's get this party started!" Jimmy Van Heusen called out as he made an entrance with three girls on each arm. Always three girls on each arm.

Jack Kennedy eye-fucked a big-titted blonde, having none of it when Sinatra recommended a petite redhead instead.

"Maybe later, Frank," he said, ready to tear into the blonde like a tornado through a trailer park.

Sinatra flashed a devilish smile. "Have you ever screwed a girl with a shaved pussy?"

Jack gave the redhead a closer look. "Really, Frank?"

"Ring-a-ding-ding!"

Jack thought back to when Frank had told him that Juliet Prowse, who starred with him in the recent movie *Can-Can*, had a shaved pussy that had sent him into orbit. Forgot about the blonde as if she weren't even there.

Sinatra watched Kennedy spring into action. *Hello. I'm Jack. Bedroom.* Zero to sixty in the blink of an eye.

George served his boss a drink.

Sinatra took a sip, then looked curiously at his valet. "From the look on your face when you were talking with Jack, I get the feeling you don't like him very much."

"I like him fine, Mr. S."

"Sit down, George. And don't bullshit me," Sinatra said as he rearranged a vase of orange gladiolas. "We've been together for seven years, and I can read you like a book."

"A president who cheats on his wife can't be trusted not to cheat the country."

"All presidents cheat on their wives, and America is doing just fine."

"Senator Kennedy is supposed to be different. He goes out of his way to put on a very liberal front, but reading between the lines, I think the apple might not have fallen far from the tree."

Sinatra knew that Jack carried the heavy burden of his father's expectations but also that he was his own man.

"Jack is nothing like his father."

"Maybe, maybe not. But he's supposed to be our hope for the future, for a better America. And as a Negro man, I need that hope, not to be stuck under the thumb of another president who is more interested in pussy than he is in my right to use a public toilet."

"Jack is different. It's a new decade."

"1960 is only a number, Mr. S. Until two months ago when the NAACP worked out an agreement with casino owners, I couldn't stay with you at the Sands. Even Sammy couldn't stay at the Sands—a headliner forced to sleep at a westside rooming house, who had to come into the hotel through the kitchen." George looked across the table at the man with whom he shared a closeness much deeper than boss and employee. "And I know the only reason the casino owners finally came around is because you stood up to them. But we still have a long way to go."

"The sad truth, George, is that away from the Strip, Vegas is still a Jim Crow town. But Jack is going to change all that."

"It takes a long time to change how people think."

"I'm going to get him elected and let him prove it to you."

They saw Jack walk back out to the pool after his quickie.

"Excuse me, Mr. S. Our hope for the future needs another daiquiri."

CHAPTER 8

Sinatra believed that Jack's campaign pledge to get the country moving forward was not just lip service. He agreed with the candidate's positions on national defense, economic growth, and a new image for America, and vowed to work his ass off to get him elected, beginning on friendly turf.

Luizzi's Tavern, the Marlin Room, and Tank's Tap were among Hoboken, New Jersey's busiest boozatoriums, and Frank and his father, Marty, hit them all, buying drinks, glad-handing, putting up posters, and handing out campaign buttons. Kennedy. Kennedy. Kennedy. All the way with JFK.

Marty Sinatra, a former boxer and bartender, was a fireman who had achieved the rank of captain as tribute to Hoboken's favorite son. But it was Frank's mother, Dolly, a former midwife and abortionist from whom Frank got his swagger, who had the political muscle. A ward heeler, she helped document Italian immigrants fresh off the boat in exchange for voting the straight Democratic ticket. She curried favor for decades with the Hoboken political machine by continually turning out that vote, this time working overtime for JFK.

As was Frank, going so far as to have songwriter Sammy Cahn write "Vote for Kennedy" lyrics for his Oscar-winning song "High Hopes":

> *Everyone is voting for Jack,*
> *'Cause he's got what all the rest lack.*
> *Everyone wants to back Jack.*
> *Jack is on the right track.*
>
> *'Cause he's got high hopes.*
> *He's got high hopes.*
> *1960's the year*
> *For his high hopes.*

Sinatra recorded a forty-five of the reworked song and put one on every jukebox in Hoboken along with a crisp $50 bill for the proprietor to play it constantly, and had mobbed-up union boss Jimmy Hoffa get his Teamsters to do the same in every bar in the state.

Joe and Pete's, Dirk's Den, and making it to the Brass Rail just before last call, they put a poster in the window, a record on the jukebox and bought drinks for everyone in the place. Working stiffs with the ooze of a hard day's work still ripe on their clothes, all of them thrilled to be hanging out with the most popular entertainer in the world.

Almost all of them.

"That a Pink Squirrel you're drinking?" yelled a drunk the size of a refrigerator.

"What's that, pal?"

"Don't all you Hollywood faggots drink Pink Squirrels?"

Frank stepped toward the big man. "Maybe you've had enough booze for one night."

"I don't need a pansy like you to tell me when I've had enough. And I sure as hell ain't gonna vote for your faggot boyfriend."

Sinatra knocked him out with one punch, pinned a JFK button on his shirt, and bought another round for the house.

CHAPTER 9

West Virginia was a heavily Protestant state with a poorly educated population that needed to be convinced that Kennedy did not answer directly to the Vatican. Impoverished people working their asses off in coal mines trying to make ends meet, with family breadwinners all too often dropping dead from black lung disease. And even though Jack was trying to push a mine safety bill through the Senate, Hubert Humphrey—endorsed by the United Mine Workers—had a big lead in the polls, leaving the rich Irish Catholic from Boston to fight with one arm tied behind his back.

Sam Giancana did as he had promised by flipping the union endorsement from Humphrey to Kennedy, but it was still a horse race, neck and neck down the stretch. And although it was comforting to know the fix was in, Sinatra believed in Jack and campaigned tirelessly to make sure he won on the legit. Down to the wire, it was anybody's race, and Sinatra was determined to be the difference maker. Not only did he put posters in store windows and records in jukeboxes, he made personal appearances and posed for pictures, getting out the Kennedy vote any way he could.

He wowed housewives coming in and out of the Foodway Key Market in Morgantown, a nothing burg hugging a bend in the Monongahela River, shaking hands and kissing babies while passing out bumper stickers and campaign buttons. He gave the eye to a pretty girl with honey-colored hair and a faint sprinkling of freckles on her nose. She was a little young for his taste but old enough to vote, so he invited her back to his hotel, then gave her a hundred-dollar bill, whispered something in her ear, and sent her into the store.

"Robbing the cradle, Frank?" snapped Bobby Kennedy, a pint-sized version of his brother who overcompensated by talking tough. "I thought it was made clear that you are not to actively campaign. Your playboy image is doing more harm than good."

"Look at these women swooning over me. They all vote. And not for who their husbands tell them to vote for. When they pull shut that curtain on election day, every one of them will vote for Jack."

Bobby Kennedy understood that a dirt-poor housewife's vote counted the same as that of a country club socialite, but that did not mean he would allow Sinatra to put the campaign at risk.

"You're a liability, Frank. An unprincipled degenerate whose very presence here stains the Kennedy name."

"Stay the fuck out of my way, little brother," Sinatra told him. "Go home and take care of those seven kids of yours while I work my magic and get Jack elected."

The honey-haired girl came out of the store carrying a small paper bag, and Bobby Kennedy fumed as he watched her walk with Sinatra down the street toward his hotel.

A sagging mattress, rabbit-eared television, and shower that dripped were a far cry from his suite at the Sands, but it was the best hotel room Morgantown had to offer. Sinatra poured them each a drink and breathed life into a Chesterfield. Sat on the edge of the bed and told the girl to take off her clothes. Inspected her as she stood naked in front of him. No mileage. Tits that stood at attention. He ran his fingers through the mound of silky hair between her legs, then rubbed his face against it. Opened the bag from the store and took out a can of shaving cream and a double-edged razor. He smiled as he led her into the bathroom.

CHAPTER 10

It was a 104 degrees at midnight as ten thousand people jammed downtown's Glitter Gulch hoping to catch a glimpse of the big names who had traveled to the desert for the world premiere of *Ocean's 11*. Away from the Strip, Las Vegas was a young town on the make, kicking the horse shit off its boots for a night in the spotlight, a spotlight Sinatra had a special reason for shining on the small Fremont Theater rather than the traditional opening-night glitz of Grauman's Chinese in Hollywood.

The stars of the movie came stag, with the exception of Sammy, who clung to his blond Swedish stunner like skin on a grape. Dean, who never seemed to take anything seriously, cracked wise and mugged for the cameras while co-stars Cesar Romero and Richard Conte soaked up the spotlight with Hollywood A-listers who Sinatra had persuaded to brave the late-summer heat by arranging for them to receive comped rooms and full VIP treatment at the Sands, all as part of his plan to get them to hop aboard the JFK Express that had been charging full speed ahead since the victory he had delivered in the West Virginia primary. A win proving to party bosses that his pal could come out on top in a heavily non-Catholic state, leading to John Fitzgerald Kennedy winning the Democratic presidential nomination on the first ballot at the convention and setting up a race for the White House against Vice President Richard Nixon. And in the morning, Frank would be back on the campaign trail shaking hands and kissing babies while passing out bumper stickers and campaign buttons. All the way with JFK.

Frank joked with Angie Dickinson, a minor television actress he had connected with over a mutual fascination with toy trains. How as kids, instead of sitting on Santa's lap, both had watched the electric trains go round and round Christmas trees in department store windows, imagining all the places real trains would one day take them. They became close but, even though she was easy on the eyes, he never had sex with her, instead becoming her pal, which was out of character, as sex had driven every relationship Sinatra had ever had with a woman. Sex was always the reason for hello, and sex with someone new was always the reason for goodbye. But Frank saw Angie as more than a plaything—a great broad with whom he could drop the bravado and relax. There was a bond of trust between them. He took her under his wing and suggested she become a blonde to help make the career leap from the small screen to the big screen, which was also out of character considering his penchant for brunettes. She took his advice, and he cast her in the role of his wife in *Ocean's 11*.

Although Sinatra was confident the movie would be a hit, he kept a close eye on the invited guests during the screening, trying to gauge if their favorable reactions were a matter of politeness or if they really did enjoy it. He eventually concluded that their responsiveness was indeed the real deal that indicated he was sitting atop a pile of box office gold. Then, after the final credits had rolled and the applause had died down, Sammy took Frank aside on their way out of the theater. Giddy as a schoolboy, he told Frank that he and May were getting married in October and asked him to be the best man.

Sinatra was honored. A romantic at heart, he was so happy for his friend that, for a moment, he forgot all about the crush of fans who, despite the heat and the late hour, were still congregated outside on Fremont Street.

CHAPTER 11

"Peter is positive we're having an affair," Pat told Sinatra as they enjoyed the cool evening breeze on the deck of the Lawford beach house in Santa Monica. Then looked inside at her husband trying to make time with an over-breasted starlet. "Though I don't think he much cares."

"A couple nights of ring-a-ding-ding is hardly an affair," Frank told the dark-haired socialite, who was dressed Ivy League casual, fondling her tits with his eyes. "But I'm all in favor of going back for another taste."

"Anytime," she smiled, playfully reaching around to pinch his ass as she saw that her house was beginning to fill up with people waiting to meet her brother.

Not just people, a throng of movie stars Sinatra had mobilized, positive that their public support would flip Jack's negative poll numbers. An affair catered by Beverly Hills restauranteur Mike Romanoff while jazz cat Gerry Mulligan and his combo provided the soundtrack, with no press and no photographers so that the candidate could let his hair down and enjoy himself. All the way with JFK. Tony

Curtis and his wife, Janet Leigh, were there, as were Gregory Peck, Henry Fonda, and a dozen other big names whose public support could put Kennedy over the top. And one who could sink the entire campaign.

Applause erupted as Jack Kennedy walked in with his brother Bobby, who was livid as he saw Marilyn Monroe and immediately pushed Peter Lawford aside.

"What the hell is she doing here?"

"Jack invited her," Lawford said in his polished British accent.

"Don't lie to me, Peter. Jack knows better than to do that."

The words rang hollow as even he knew that his brother was so pussy-whipped that he did *not* know better than to do that. No matter how many times Bobby had warned him that, as a married man, he needed to stay away from Marilyn, Jack continued to see her whenever he could, not seeming to care that being caught with her even once would ruin any chance he had of becoming president. There were already whispers of an affair, but if the who's who of Hollywood elite saw Jack and Marilyn cozying up together at the party, or god forbid sneaking off together, the gossip generated would quickly make headlines.

"They're pretty good, don't you think, Senator?" asked Kirk Douglas, nodding toward the combo.

"Jack. Call me Jack."

"So, what do you think of them, Jack?"

"To be honest, I see jazz as being a lot like Congress in how all the musicians seem to be playing a different song at the same time."

"I hear you're a sailor," Orson Welles said. "I have a forty-five-foot ketch at Marina del Rey. Love to take you out sometime."

"Just tell me when, Orson."

"Would it be in poor taste if I told a Polack joke?" Paul Newman asked.

"Hell no." Jack laughed. "In Washington, we call them Russian jokes."

And so it went. A love fest with everyone wanting a piece of the candidate.

None more so than Marilyn, who had not yet made a move toward Jack as he continued to circulate. And it was Bobby's job to make sure that she did not. A job that became increasingly more difficult as Marilyn grew impatient, chasing vodka with gin as she waited for the man she had fallen so hard for, the white knight who would rescue her from the emptiness that was eroding her soul, the man who had told her that he loved her and who, she believed, would divorce his wife after the election and marry her.

"This is all your fault, Frank," Bobby snarled.

"Fuck off," Pat snapped at her brother. "Frank didn't invite her."

"But he is *supposed* to be Jack's friend." His eyes shot daggers at Sinatra. "And if you care at all about seeing him in the White House, you'll get Marilyn the hell out of here. And you'll do it right now before something happens."

"Okay, Bobby," Frank told him. "I'll have my driver take her home."

"Just like that? No argument?"

"When you're right, you're right."

Bobby Kennedy was stunned. Could not believe his eyes as Sinatra made his way across the room and quietly spirited Marilyn out the door.

"Maybe now you'll finally see what a good man Frank is," Pat told him. "And that he has nothing but our brother's best interest at heart."

"I heard Dad say once that even a broken watch is right twice a day. But beyond that, the reality is that Frank Sinatra does not care about anyone except Frank Sinatra."

Hollywood's biggest stars fawned over the man *Time* hailed as a new breed who offered America a breath of fresh air and *Newsweek* called the candidate of the future. It was admiration that, to Jack, seemed misdirected, as to him movie stars were the ones with the power to hold the world in the palm of their hands. Presidents were admired by half the country while movie stars were beloved around the globe, but who was he to question the workings of the world when knockout Kim Novak slipped him her number and James Garner invited him to play golf?

Sipping Pepsi-Cola through a straw, Bobby continued to keep a protective eye on his brother. And with the shindig still in full swing, he followed Jack to the bathroom and stood guard outside the door to make sure he didn't try to sneak out with his dick pointing in the direction of Marilyn's house—unaware that Jack had already climbed out the window and hailed a cab.

A clean getaway.

Except for the fact that there had been a photographer lurking in the bushes.

CHAPTER 12

"I, uh, just went out to get some fresh air," Jack stammered, caught off guard by his brother as he entered his hotel suite just past dawn.

"Lie to the voters, lie to your wife, but don't lie to me. Don't you *ever* lie to me!" Bobby handed him an envelope. "This was delivered an hour ago."

Jack opened it to find a photograph of himself climbing out of the Lawfords' bathroom window and another of him getting into a cab. Then the coup de grace of him getting out of the same cab in front of Marilyn's house.

"I can explain."

"No, you can't. And right now, we have a bigger problem, because the man who took these photographs is going to call in a few minutes and demand money."

"Pay him."

"Don't be stupid, Jack. This guy could extort your presidency for the next eight years."

"You're overreacting, Bobby. He's probably just an opportunist looking to make a quick buck."

"We can't take that chance. If these photos got into the wrong hands, not only would you lose the election but your entire political future would go down the drain. Not to mention, you would also lose your family, including Caroline and the new baby on the way, because Jackie will not stand for any sort of public humiliation." Bobby was furious, but that did not mean he had stopped caring. "Is Marilyn really worth losing all that?"

Jack grinned.

Bobby blew his top.

"You think this is a blasted joke? If that blond bimbo does anything else to jeopardize your future, I will personally see to it that *she* doesn't have one."

"Leave Marilyn alone."

"You leave Marilyn alone."

"It's my life, little brother."

"Then open your eyes and see what's at stake."

"Don't you think I know that Jackie is the most wonderful woman in the world?"

"Then why do you cheat on her?"

"It's not cheating because Jackie has my heart. But it's not enough. I need more. I need it all, and sleeping with other women is how I stay true to myself."

"You screw these sluts to feed your ego?"

"I wouldn't expect you to understand."

"Is that why you want to be president? Because you want people to like you?"

"I want to be president to preserve democracy by ending the Communist threat. I want to make sure that every American has the right to a good education and a decent living wage. And I want history to remember me by what I accomplished, not by whom I slept with."

"And Jackie isn't enough for you?"

"When I'm in bed with her, I think about that stacked brunette Judy Campbell. And when I'm with Judy, I think about Marilyn, and when I'm with Marilyn, I think about Jackie."

"Then forget all the other women and be faithful to your wife."

"You haven't heard a word I've said."

"Go clean yourself up while I figure out the best way to handle this. And wear a bright-colored tie because you're speaking at the Women's Charity League luncheon in Pasadena."

Bobby paced the room, his brain firing on all cylinders but coming up empty as he searched for a way out of the mess his brother had gotten himself into. A way out that should have been in his back pocket long ago in anticipation of a moment like this that he had always feared would one day come.

Jack showered and was finished dressing when the call came, and the price to buy the photos and negatives was $50,000 to be paid that night with further instructions to follow. He told his brother to arrange for the money.

"How can we be sure he won't keep copies to blackmail you with later?"

"It's a chance we'll have to take," Jack said. "What else can we do?"

Bobby was not about to chance trusting a blackmailer. Wheels turning as he tried to figure another way.

"Maybe you were right when you said he's just an opportunist looking to make a quick buck, because if he had half a brain, he would have already sold these photos to Nixon for twice the money," Bobby reasoned. "And it would not even have been illegal."

"Then let's give him the money and be done with it."

"But what if the reason he didn't go to Nixon is because he could have collected only once?" Bobby saw potential disaster no matter what they decided to do. He picked up the phone. "I'm calling Dad. He got you out of a paternity claim and two breach of promise suits back when you were a congressman."

"By buying off the women. I thought you didn't want to pay for the pictures."

"I don't. There's a better way."

"And just what would that be?"

"I don't know, but it's for sure Dad will."

CHAPTER 13

The Astor Arts Theater was a small movie house that screened obscure avant-garde films to even smaller audiences in West Los Angeles. A man in his early thirties, wearing a corduroy jacket and brown slacks, sat at a bus stop across the street, continually checking his watch and looking both ways.

"Afraid I wasn't coming?" asked a man in a dark suit and gray hat as he sat beside him.

"Afraid I'd miss the last show that starts in twenty minutes." He looked at the man seated beside him. "Do you have my money?"

The man removed a thick envelope from his inside pocket and fanned through the bills, pulling it back as the photographer reached for it.

"First things first," he said, then shook his head as he noticed that the Astor Arts marquee read *Peeping Tom*. "It figures."

"I'm not a pervert, if that's what you think. It's a British film about a cameraman stalking women while making a documentary about fear. Guy put a mirrored contraption on his movie camera to make them see their own terror as he murders them."

"These women watch themselves getting killed?"

"That's right. The film is groundbreaking. Director Michael Powell is way ahead of his time."

Only an idiot would have a casual conversation about an art house film during a blackmail payoff, and the man with the money needed to cut to the chase.

"Give me the photographs and negatives."

He handed them over.

The man in the suit did not bother to ask if there were any other copies because an accomplice had already searched the photographer's apartment and studio. Then the assassin Sam Giancana had sent slid a knife into the blackmailer's heart and propped him up on the bench as if he were waiting for a bus. He started to walk away, then again noticed the marquee. Women watching themselves being murdered? Why not?

He crossed the street and bought a ticket in plenty of time to catch the last show.

CHAPTER 14

Nearing the end of September, the polls had the Democratic ticket of John F. Kennedy and Lyndon Johnson six points behind Nixon and Lodge, a deficit Sinatra could not for the life of him understand. Jack was charismatic, handsome and had a vision for the future. Nixon was yesterday's news, having been Eisenhower's vice president for eight years. Beady-eyed. Always looked like he needed a shave. And if he rose to power, America would be stuck in the 1950s forever.

Sinatra raked in major donations and turned out crowds at campaign rallies from Syracuse to San Diego, sometimes with the candidate and sometimes with Lawford, who had recently become a naturalized citizen so he could vote for his brother-in-law. Frank had appeared at a few select events with Sammy, but he never campaigned with Dean. Dean liked Jack well enough, but politics bored him, and he did not care who sat in the Oval Office as long as he was free to carouse and play golf.

Tonight, Sinatra was in Chicago with Sam Giancana in a secure suite at the Palmer House, where they would watch the first-ever televised presidential debate in a few minutes, aired live from the

WBBM-TV studio down the street. He was confident that Jack would win the debate, but racked his brain trying to figure out what more could be done to flip the poll numbers.

"I just don't know what else I can do, Sam."

"Don't worry about it," Giancana told him as he inspected the lit end of his cigar, then leaned back on the sofa and smiled. "Even the best magician in the world can't pull a rabbit out of a hat unless there is already a rabbit in the hat."

Sinatra looked curiously at the gangster who, since day one, had been sweating every last detail but was all of a sudden relaxed. Happy. Almost giddy.

"And you have a rabbit in your hat?" Sinatra asked.

"I always have a rabbit in my hat."

"What did you do, Sam?"

"I guaranteed our boy a landslide victory in November, and it only cost me a hundred bucks."

"Please tell me you didn't do anything that could backfire."

Giancana busted out laughing.

"Dammit, Sam. You're making me nervous."

"I bribed a stagehand to spike Nixon's coffee with a horse laxative just before he goes on." Barely able to contain his glee, Giancana got up and turned on the television. "And when he shits all over every TV set in America, our man Kennedy will win the election in a walk."

The candidates took the stage with CBS newsman Howard K. Smith moderating.

Opening statements.

Voters from coast to coast hanging on every word.

The gangster and the singer watching Nixon. Waiting for the fireworks.

Questions.

"Senator Kennedy, why should the federal government continue to pay farmers not to grow certain crops?"

"Mr. Vice President, you have said that you have more government executive decision-making experience, yet President Eisenhower, when asked to provide an example, could not produce a single one. Can *you* give us an example?"

"Senator Kennedy, you are calling for expansion of welfare programs while at the same time reducing federal debt. How do you plan to pay the bill for all that spending?"

Answers and rebuttals. Two heavyweights going toe to toe. Kennedy looking composed, whereas Nixon, who had refused makeup, came off as pale and sickly under the studio lights while he fidgeted and sweated profusely.

The two men at the Palmer House waited for the explosion. Any minute. Any second.

"Mr. Vice President, you have called for higher salaries for teachers, yet you refused to break a tie in the Senate that would have granted those increases. Could you explain that, sir?"

Giancana was on the edge of his seat as Nixon was doing a masterful job of holding it in.

"Senator Kennedy, you have promised, if elected, to push through bills on medical aid to the aged and a comprehensive minimum wage of $1.25 an hour. You previously could not get action on these bills in Congress, so how do you feel you will be able to do so as president?"

Answers and rebuttals.

Giancana pacing.

Nixon somehow keeping it together in front of the cameras, even though the churning laxative made him look jittery and out of sorts while his polished opponent exhibited the composure of a statesman.

Closing statements.

Kennedy poised and standing tall.

Nixon grimacing, ready to blow any second as he uncomfortably shifted his weight from side to side.

"Shit, you motherfucker!" Giancana yelled at the television. "SHIT!"

The debate was over.

"You are dead!" Giancana screamed. "You are motherfucking dead!"

The candidates shook hands, and as the vice president raced to the toilet, the gangster fired six bullets into the picture tube.

Sinatra waited a moment for Giancana to calm down, then put things into perspective.

"You gave Jack the win by making Nixon look like a junkie who needed a fix."

"I didn't want to win just the debate, Frank. If Nixon had shit his pants, the election would have been ours in a landslide."

"The important thing is that Jack is now the front-runner," Sinatra said as he lit a Chesterfield.

"I guess you're right," Giancana agreed, as even though it was not the spectacular knockout he had wanted, it still counted as a win. "And I have to tell you that making a difference with a little hands-on fuckery feels pretty goddam good. I think I'll pull a few more rabbits out of my hat before November."

Sinatra blew a smoke ring and smiled. "Let's get a couple broads up here and celebrate."

Everything was aces until they woke up to the morning edition of the *Chicago Tribune* and discovered that while people watching on television saw Kennedy as the winner of the debate, those listening on the radio did not see Nixon's painstaking effort to keep from shitting himself and felt that he had been the clear winner. Fortunately for Kennedy, television was fast becoming the medium for the new decade, and he had managed to erase the six-point deficit, racing toward election day with the candidates locked in a dead heat.

CHAPTER 15

Being back in Vegas for a run of Rat Pack shows at the Sands felt like a vacation for Sinatra following a campaign swing of sixteen cities in twenty-two days as he unwound with the usual suspects in his dressing room before heading out for a late supper at Villa d'Este, a high-end Italian restaurant in the backyard of the Strip that Joseph "Joe the Cook" Pignatello fronted for Sam Giancana because of his inclusion on the Nevada Gaming Control Board's List of Excluded Persons. The restaurant was as close as the gangster could get to any casino without being hauled out in handcuffs.

Angie Dickinson looked like a million in a snug-fitting knit dress. May and Sammy nuzzled on the sofa, while Lawford put the moves on a stunning off-duty showgirl.

"Excuse me, doll," Frank said to the gorgeous redhead Lawford was trying to make time with. "Do you mind if I borrow my friend for a second?"

"I'll be right back," Lawford told her, then followed Sinatra to a corner, where they huddled with Dean. "If this is about your idea of changing the name of the act to Franks and Deans, your timing is lousy."

"It's about that girl," Dean told him.

"She have the clap or something?"

Dean shook his head. "Nothing like that."

"Then what are you trying to tell me? That you slept with her? Because I don't care."

Dean gave Frank a pained look. "I can't tell him."

"He has to know before it's too late."

"Too late for what?" Lawford demanded. "Will you guys quit beating around the bush and tell me what the hell is going on?"

"You don't want her, Charlie," Sinatra told him.

"The hell I don't. Look at her."

Dean grabbed an eyeful. Hair. Tits. Legs. Wow.

"Either tell me right now or I'm taking that sweet piece of ass up to my room," Lawford said.

"She fucked Milton Berle's German shepherd," Sinatra told him.

"Very funny." Lawford was furious that his friends were trying to muck up his chance with a perfect ten. "You clowns are a million laughs."

But he saw they weren't laughing.

"Berle has pictures," Dean told him, his expression serious as a heart attack. "The other night, he was showing them to everyone over at the Flame."

Lawford walked away, past the perfect ten without a word and out the door.

Frank and Dean busted out laughing, then Dean walked over to the showgirl, who knew they had been talking about her and wanted to know what was so funny.

"Just playing a little joke on a pal." Dean smiled and handed her a drink.

"Thanks, but I never touch it."

He looked at her as if she had three heads.

"You're a Vegas showgirl and you don't drink?"

"Nope."

"You a Mormon?"

"Hell no. I just prefer to see the world through clear eyes."

"Oh, baby. You don't know what you're missing. Because when you wake up in the morning, that's as good as you're gonna feel all day."

"I doubt that," the showgirl smiled, nibbling his ear as she ran her fingers up his trouser leg.

Sinatra poured refills for himself and Angie, who matched him drink for drink, a quality he admired in a woman. They toasted *Ocean's 11*, which had become a box office hit despite mixed reviews. As they talked about future projects, a distinguished figure walked through the door.

"Mr. Ambassador," Sinatra called out as he flashed a big smile to Joe Kennedy, who was undoubtedly there to express his gratitude for the nonstop campaigning that was about to get his son elected president of the United States. "What a pleasant surprise. Did you see the show?"

"Don't be ridiculous," he snapped, glaring at Sammy and May, who even after months together looked like lovesick teenagers. "I'm here to tell you to call off that abomination of a wedding."

"You can't be serious," Sinatra said.

"The candidates are even in the polls, and you, who have publicly positioned yourself as Jack's close friend, cannot be seen condoning interracial marriage."

"I am working my ass off to get Jack elected," Sinatra said. "And there is no goddam way I'm going to let you barge in here and tell me what to do."

"Don't take that tone with me."

"I'll say the same to you."

"If you stand up as best man at the wedding of a white girl and a nigger—a nigger Jew, no less—the Republicans will have a field day." He looked at Sammy and shook his head. "What sort of imbecile would *choose* to be a fucking Jew?"

Sinatra glared at the old man. "The wedding goes on as scheduled."

"Will you at least tell him to postpone that obscenity until after the election?"

"I won't hurt a friend."

"Even if it means giving that bastard Nixon the White House?"

"The wedding goes on as scheduled," Sinatra repeated.

"I'm warning you. There are severe consequences for crossing a Kennedy."

"Don't threaten me, old man."

"You will regret this, Francis." Joe Kennedy looked at Sammy and May with disgust. "I'll tell the little kike myself."

CHAPTER 16

"Louise, have you seen my silver tie clasp?" Joe Pulitzer called loudly from the bedroom. "Louise!"

A man in his late forties, Pulitzer never left the house without being immaculately turned out, and continued to search with no luck.

"Louise!"

No answer came, so he selected a different tie clasp, stood before a full-length mirror, and proclaimed himself good to go for another day as publisher of the *St. Louis Post-Dispatch*. He was hungry for his breakfast that was on the table at precisely the same time every morning, but as he walked down the stairs, he was not greeted by the usual aroma of sausage and eggs. He stepped into the kitchen to find his wife sitting at the table with a man holding a gun to her head.

Pulitzer's eyes widened. "Take whatever you want, just don't hurt her."

"This is not a robbery."

"Then what do you want?" Pulitzer demanded of the man in a conservative business suit who, except for the gun in his hand, looked as if he might have stopped by to sell insurance. "Never mind. I'm calling the police."

The gunman pulled back the hammer of his .38.

"It's no secret that your newspaper is expected to endorse Nixon this week."

"What of it? I think Richard Nixon is the better candidate."

"No, you don't."

"I absolutely do, and so does the public, as evidenced by the massive crowd who showed up to greet him at the airport when he was in town last month for a campaign speech."

"Your old lady has a gun to her head and you want to argue politics?"

"Kennedy is nothing more than a dilettante, while Nixon has the experience of eight years as vice president and a firm grasp on how to offset rising government spending while avoiding the hazards of inflation."

"Joe!" screamed his terrified wife. "Shut up and do whatever he wants."

"Here is how it's going to be," the gunman told him. "You are going to call your editor and tell him that you won't be in today, but that you want him to run an endorsement of John F. Kennedy on the front page of the afternoon edition and that the copy will be delivered to his office at exactly nine o'clock."

"I won't do it. The *Post-Dispatch* has been a beacon of honesty and integrity throughout the state of Missouri since my grandfather put out the first edition in 1878."

"Make the call or your wife dies." The gunman pressed the barrel of his weapon against Louise's forehead.

"Joe, please! Do what he says!"

For all his bravado, Joe Pulitzer saw no way out, so he picked up the wall extension and called his editor with the instructions. It was a call that was met with both surprise and resistance.

"I've changed my mind, that's all... Yes, I'm sure I want to do this... I don't need to defend my editorial policy to anyone, including you... Just run the endorsement word for word, above the fold, or tomorrow you'll be looking for another job!" He slammed down the phone and faced the gunman. "I did what you wanted, now get out of here and leave us alone."

"Just as soon as the afternoon edition hits the street." He lowered his gun and told Louise to put on a pot of coffee and make some bacon and eggs.

"We don't have any bacon," she said nervously. "Joe likes sausage."

"Then by all means fry up some sausage. After switching his political affiliation, I think Joe has earned it."

"You're just a hired thug, so I wouldn't expect you to understand, or even care, about the harm you are doing by trying to subvert this election."

"One more word and I'll put a bullet through your teeth."

For several hours, the three of them sat at the kitchen table watching the clock tick. The silence was unnerving. Louise made lunch, and then they went into the living room to wait for the paperboy, who would roll by with the afternoon edition right after school was out.

It took what seemed like forever, but finally, out the window, they saw the bicycle as the boy tossed the newspaper onto the front porch.

"Go and get it," the gunman instructed.

Pulitzer did as he was told. Came back inside and closed the door, grimacing as he saw the front page. The gunman grabbed the paper, then enjoyed watching the arrogant publisher die a little with each word as he read the endorsement out loud.

"The *St. Louis Post-Dispatch*, speaking as an independent newspaper, today announces its support of John Fitzgerald Kennedy for president. Although this announcement may come as a surprise to many, two considerations have carried special weight in determining our judgment. One of these is a matter of foreign policy. The other is a question of ensuring a unified direction of the nation's affairs at a difficult moment in history."

There were several more paragraphs about the imperialist-Communist threat, Kennedy's ability to bridge a divisive Congress, and blah, blah, blah, who cares? Nobody would read that far anyway. The point already made, as all people would remember is the newspaper that stood for honesty and integrity throughout the state of Missouri had told them to vote for Kennedy.

CHAPTER 17

On election night at his Wonder Palms estate, Sinatra watched the results with Jimmy Van Heusen and a few of the fellas. Hookers were on call but not until victory was assured.

Jimmy sat at the piano while Frank sang:

Everyone is voting for Jack,
'Cause he's got what all the rest lack.
Everyone wants to back Jack.
Jack is on the right track.

The others gathered around and loudly joined in the chorus.

'Cause he's got high hopes.
He's got high hopes.
1960's the year
For his high hopes.

Come on and vote for Kennedy.
Vote for Kennedy,
And we'll come out on top...
Oops, there goes the opposition—ker...
Oops, there goes the opposition—ker,
Oops, there goes the opposition.
KERPLOP!

Again and again, middle-aged men sang with the enthusiasm of teenagers until they worked up a thirst that needed to be satisfied. George served drinks while Sinatra looked at his watch.

"It's going to be a while until they declare Jack the winner, so we may as well have a little fun while we wait." He smiled at Jimmy. "Call the girls and get them over here."

Booze, broads, and election coverage on Frank's state-of-the-art twenty-one-inch Magnavox. But while his pals scattered for a little ring-a-ding-ding, Sinatra stayed glued to NBC News as John Chancellor reported incidental results of John H. Reed and Wesley Powell being re-elected governors of Maine and New Hampshire, respectively, just in case there might be a presidential update. But that did not prevent him from letting the cute brunette nuzzling up to him on the sofa unzip his trousers and dive in for some good old-fashioned skull-fucking.

Kennedy carried major states New York, Pennsylvania, and Texas, as well as toss-up states Missouri, Georgia, and Minnesota, where Giancana had extorted major newspaper endorsements. Nixon grabbed the prize in Ohio while nickel-and-diming electoral votes in a majority of the smaller states, leaving the voters of Illinois, as most had predicted, to decide who would become the next president of the United States. Sinatra had wanted so desperately for Jack to win fair and square, and had honestly believed he would, but as the night dragged on, it became obvious that the outcome was in Giancana's hands.

Nixon carried rural and downstate Illinois, but Chicago returns trickled in slowly, and the fellas, who had already gotten their rocks off, left Sinatra to wait alone for confirmation of a Kennedy victory. *A fixed election should not go down to the wire,* he thought, but he still had every confidence in the anticipated result. Thrilled that his pal was going to be president, that the Feds would leave the Outfit alone, and that both would owe it all to him.

John Sparkman and Gordon Allott were re-elected to the Senate from Alabama and Colorado, but who the fuck cared?

"Make the presidential race official and declare a winner!" Frank yelled at the television.

And then, just after midnight, John Chancellor all but did just that by predicting that Richard Nixon would become the next president.

Sinatra screamed until he tired himself out, switched off the television, then sat on the sofa for the next two hours staring at nothing, racking his brain to understand how it could have possibly gone wrong.

The telephone rang.

"It's Mr. Sam," George told him.

"Not now," said Sinatra, in no hurry to incur the gangster's rage. "Tell him I'll talk to him tomorrow."

"I'm sorry, Mr. S., but he insists."

Sinatra took a slug of Jack Daniel's, then grabbed the phone.

"You can't blame me for this, Sam. I did everything I could. More than anybody could ever expect."

Giancana told him to shut up and listen.

Sinatra braced for the worst, instead hearing a man who was again quick with a laugh as he told Sinatra that the Chicago wards he controlled had turned the vote count on its ass. Kennedy had the twenty-seven Illinois electoral votes in his pocket, meaning that even if Nixon won his home state of California, it was enough to put Jack over the top. The only problem was that Nixon refused to concede, meaning it would probably be late into the morning before Jack could make his victory speech.

At 3:00 a.m. Sinatra called the Ambassador Hotel in Los Angeles to demand that Nixon concede, but the operator refused to put the call through.

"This is Frank Sinatra!" he raged. "Ring his fucking room!"

The operator hung up, leaving him, like the rest of the country, to wait a few more hours. But what were a few hours when his best friend was about to become the thirty-fifth president of the United States?

CHAPTER 18

Two months had passed since the inauguration, and Frank kept busy. His foot on the gas as he prepared to shoot *The Devil at 4 O'Clock* with one of his acting idols, Spencer Tracy, and had begun pre-production on a Rat Pack Western called *Sergeants 3*. He cranked out a new LP on his Reprise label and continued to perform at the Sands. Plus nonstop booze and broads—always nonstop booze and broads—but tonight, he opened Wonder Palms for his kids to have a party.

Tina was pushing 13, Frank Jr. was 17, and 20-year-old Nancy, with a serious boyfriend, had Frank worried that she was growing up too fast. So, it made him happy that she was there with her younger siblings, a new generation that spun the latest forty-fives while laughing and joking with their friends. George served pizza and soft drinks, though allowed Nancy to sneak some vodka, while Frank, like a good parent, stayed out of the way, though not before taking photographs of the kids dancing to *their* music.

It was innocent fun, the kind of fun Sinatra had never known growing up on the downside of privilege in blue-collar Hoboken, though his mother had always managed a few extra bucks to provide him with nice clothes and other advantages the rest of the neighborhood kids didn't have. She called in favors to get him performing gigs at local social clubs, leading to a job as a singing waiter before finding success with bandleaders Harry James and Tommy Dorsey on the way to punching his ticket to the big time.

Sinatra retreated to his darkroom, though it was not far enough down the hall to escape the racket from the stack of records that drove him nuts: Del Shannon, Chuck Berry, Freddy "Boom Boom" Cannon, Dick Dale, Jackie Wilson, and, of course, Elvis Presley. And how Frank hated Elvis Presley, regarding him as a degenerate redneck and musical abomination. He had gone so far as to write a magazine article for *Western World* where he called rock and roll the ugliest and most brutal form of expression it had ever been his displeasure to hear. But Frank loved his kids, and their fun was his pleasure. So, when the party ended, he gave each of the teenage guests an album with color prints of the photos he had taken and developed earlier.

Though, throughout all of it, his thoughts never strayed far from his best pal. Frank understood that the new president was busy transitioning the government, but he still felt a bit slighted that his friend had not made time for him. Especially since he knew that Jack had more than once found the time to sneak Marilyn into the Lincoln bedroom. Far less understanding was Sam Giancana, who still walked around with a roll of dimes in his pocket.

CHAPTER 19

"You're up early, Mr. S.," remarked George as his boss greeted a new day. "Can I make you some breakfast?"

"Just coffee, George." For Sinatra's money, George made the best coffee in the world. "I'm going to get a little sun, so serve it by the pool. And bring the newspaper."

As he often did, Frank had met a few friends for dinner at Melvyn's, a happening downtown spot, the night before. But as he almost never did, he went home early and got a good night's sleep, leaving him refreshed as he perused the front page of the *Desert Sun*. Palm Springs was a small town with small news, and he read that the Los Angeles Angels expansion baseball team would be playing a spring-training game down the road that afternoon against the Chicago Cubs. Then he continued on to a photo of his neighbor, former President Eisenhower, boarding a plane to Baja to do some fishing. Looking at the duffers on the seventeenth fairway, he thought about taking a rare day off and considered getting up a foursome. Or maybe going to the ballgame. Or maybe just enjoying the peace and quiet of doing nothing.

"Good morning, Frank," said Peter Lawford, looking dapper as usual in a light-blue suit and open-collared shirt, as he joined Sinatra by the pool.

Best-laid plans...

He could see that Lawford was nervous, clinging to a rolled-up magazine in his hand.

"To what do I owe the pleasure of a morning visit?" Frank asked. "Did Joe Kennedy have another stroke?"

"I think one massive stroke was quite enough for him. He's in a wheelchair. He can't speak, and the right side of his body is completely paralyzed."

"Sit down, Charlie," Sinatra said, noticing that Lawford was sweating despite the cool morning breeze. "And tell me what you came here to say."

He placed the scandal magazine he was holding on the table between them, and Frank glanced down at the headline.

SINATRA CAUGHT IN BED WITH HIGH SCHOOL GIRL

Sinatra smashed his coffee cup as he looked at a doctored cover photo of himself with a young cheerleader, plus other phony images of him and the girl in compromising positions.

SINATRA TEEN LOVE NEST

CHEERLEADER HAVING FRANK'S BABY

"It's bullshit! Total fucking bullshit!"

"You didn't screw her?"

"Of course, I fucking screwed her. In some fleabag hotel in West Virginia. But she was no teenager. That girl was 23, and I can prove it."

"I suppose you asked to see her driver's license."

"Goddam right, I did," Sinatra said as he ripped the magazine in half. "And maybe you should start doing the same with all that young stuff you stick your dick in."

Sinatra was the undisputed king of showbiz, but there were certain members of the press who delighted in any opportunity to take a whack at him, even if they had to skew a few facts to do it. But this was an out-and-out fake from top to bottom.

"Who wrote this bullshit story?" Sinatra raged as he lit a cigarette. "I'll sue the motherfucker for everything he has."

"Take a breath, Frank, or *you* will have a stroke."

"I'll go to his house and beat the shit out of him. Then I'll make him watch while I fuck his wife. Then I'll beat the shit out of him again."

"I know it's bullshit, Frank, and so does Jack. But he needs you to keep your distance until this blows over."

"No fucking way he said that."

Sinatra stormed inside and picked up the telephone.

"The White House operator won't put the call through," Lawford said nervously.

"I got him elected for chrissakes!"

George poured Jack Daniel's over ice and handed it to his boss.

"And I threw him the greatest inauguration gala this country has ever seen, with the biggest stars in show business: Gene Kelly, Ella Fitzgerald, Nat King Cole, Laurence Olivier. Everybody who was anybody was on that stage with me."

Except Sammy Davis Jr., George thought as he listened to his boss rant. First the Kennedys made him postpone his wedding until after the election, then, to rub salt in the wound, three days before the inauguration the president-elect had his secretary call and disinvite Sammy from all official events. Making it clear to George that his hope for the future was nothing but a rotten apple that had indeed not fallen far from the Joe Kennedy tree. That Jack Kennedy used people to get what he wanted and was just like all who had come before him, more interested in chasing pussy than allowing his twenty million colored brothers and sisters to use a public restroom or drinking fountain.

"After all the promises that I would always be welcome at the White House," Sinatra continued to rage. "In the two months since he's been living there, I haven't been invited once. He sat right here in this room and told me that I would have an open invitation. My best friend, and now he won't even take my call!"

"It's Jackie's doing," Lawford said. "You know she doesn't like you, Frank."

"Stuck-up bitch."

"And Bobby. You know he's never wanted you anywhere near Jack. Even Joe distanced himself from you before his stroke. What happened to make him turn against you?"

"Fuck that old man. He got what he deserved. But what I don't understand is what that prick Bobby has against me. I've never done anything to him."

"Bobby has starch in his shorts. Pat says he's always been that way, even as a kid."

"It's more than that. And it has nothing to do with the election because he had it in for me long before I became part of the campaign."

"I don't know what to tell you, Frank, except that ever since he was appointed attorney general, he's been like a dog with a bone. He even tries to keep *me* away from Jack."

"Cut the shit, errand boy. You think I don't know you've been shooting off your mouth to anybody who'll listen about all the chippies you screw in the Lincoln bedroom?"

Sinatra stood over Lawford with his fist clenched.

"Tell Jack to call me."

"Okay, Frank. Okay." Lawford cringed. "It won't do any good, but I'll tell him."

CHAPTER 20

"Every one of these stiffs voted for Kennedy. Some of them three or four times," Sam Giancana said as he and Sinatra stood among the gravestones at St. Bloodrick's Cemetery, their topcoats offering little protection against a biting wind gusting through the gloom off Lake Michigan. "And every Hebe buried at Ridgelawn–Beth El voted for Kennedy. Winos on Skid Row were bussed from precinct to precinct and got a fin every time they voted for Kennedy. And after two goddam years in office, we still don't have a fucking thing to show for it."

"You could have told me that in a warm bar," Sinatra said against the chill.

"We got that Irish prick elected, Frank. And, not only did he welsh on the deal to take the pressure off but he did the exact opposite by making his weasel brother attorney general and turning up the heat."

"Jack has been in so far over his head dealing with the Cuban missile crisis, South Vietnam, and church bombings in Alabama, I don't think he knows the extent that Bobby is pushing this." Sinatra rubbed his hands together for warmth. "And since the old man's stroke, Bobby doesn't think he has to honor the deal."

"It was *before* the stroke that the old man sicced that weasel on us." The cigar in the corner of Giancana's mouth went out, and he threw it against a gravestone. "Joe Kennedy straight-up fucked us, like he had some sort of personal ax to grind, and now that he's a fucking vegetable, we'll never know what it was."

"I'll talk to Jack and get him to make things right."

"How? Since those scandal headlines two years ago, you've been persona non grata at the White House."

"Says who?"

"Judy Campbell, a broad I'm slipping it to who's also screwing Kennedy."

"Does Jack know that?"

"According to you, he doesn't even know what his brother is doing."

"And just so you know, Sam, that girl in West Virginia was 23."

"I don't give a fuck if she was 10. What I do give a fuck about is you getting the Kennedys to honor the fucking deal."

"I understand, Sam."

"You had better fucking understand, because the Outfit is taking it in the ass more than ever, and in today's paper, that goddam weasel was bragging about exposing union corruption and saying he's creating an organized crime section of the Justice Department that will launch a full-scale attack on what he called a 'conspiracy of evil.' The motherfucking son of a bitch called us evil!" Giancana noticed a bundled-up old woman placing flowers on a grave marked *O'Shaughnessy* in the next row. "Fucking cabbage eaters don't have sense enough to wait for a warm day."

"Bobby lashes out because he's frustrated. What do you expect from a guy who's only gotten laid seven times in his entire life?"

"All I know is that the Kennedys took from us, then went on the attack. Feds in cheap suits follow me everywhere I go. And don't tell me I'm being paranoid, because now those cockroaches even follow me into the fucking men's room." The wind blew out the match as Giancana tried to light another cigar. Took him two more tries to get it going. "And it all goes back to Joe. As soon as we gave him the one thing he wanted more than anything else in the world, he turned on us. What changed, Frank? What do you know about it?"

There are severe consequences for crossing a Kennedy.

Sinatra could hear the words like it was yesterday, but he had figured that the old man had just been posturing. How could he have known that an argument about Sammy's wedding would lead to an escalated attack?

"All I know is that when I brought you the old man's proposition, the first thing you said was that he was a liar and couldn't be trusted."

The gangster's eyes narrowed. "You saying this is my fault?"

"Of course not, Sam," Sinatra answered quickly, then took a breath to compose himself. "I'm saying that your first instinct was correct. A leopard can't change his spots, and he proved that by fucking us over."

"Us? What do you mean *us*? You're still making movies and records while we're losing a fucking fortune." He stepped toward Sinatra, backing him against a gravestone. "The Outfit wants *you* held accountable."

"Me? Why me?"

"Jack is *your* guy, Frank. You brought him to us, and that's why we're not talking in some warm bar. I want to make sure I have your full attention."

"None of this is my fault, Sam."

"Tell that to Carlos Marcello. He wants to feed you to the alligators, and a lot of the other bosses want to watch him do it. You brokered the deal and told us we could trust the Kennedys. You vouched for Jack, and that makes you responsible."

Sinatra could not believe that the gangster's rage, something he had once cautioned Joe Kennedy to be careful of, was now aimed at him.

"Don't worry, Sam," Sinatra told him.

"For two goddam years you've been telling me not to worry, and now it's time for *you* to worry."

"Jack will come through," Sinatra said, needing to believe it.

"When? It seems to me that a man in charge of running an entire country should be able to control his own brother. Especially a brother who fucking works for him." The gangster turned his back to the wind. "That fucking weasel still has taps on all my phones and bugs in all my broads' apartments and everywhere I hang out, so you had better make sure he does come through. And quick, because I'm just about out of patience."

Sinatra looked closely at him, and for the first time in all the years he had known Sam Giancana, he did not see a friend. He saw a killer. A killer who would soon take aim at him unless he could make things right.

"I'll talk to Jack and tell him to make Bobby back off."

"How are you going to do that when you can't even get the son of a bitch on the phone?"

CHAPTER 21

Jack Kennedy relaxed in his boxer shorts in the master bedroom of the presidential suite on the twenty-sixth floor of New York's Carlyle Hotel, going over notes for a speech he was going to deliver the following morning at the United Nations. Even before he was elected, the president had been partial to the timeless luxury of the Carlyle, a preferred landing spot for the global elite. Long known for protecting the privacy of its guests to the point of allowing certain young ladies to be escorted into the hotel through a secret system of tunnels that could only be accessed through an unmarked doorway across the street.

The stress of a long day was taking its toll as he tried to figure out the most effective way to stare down the premier of the Soviet Union, Nikita Khrushchev, who continued to make noise about escalating the Cold War into a nuclear game of chicken. Kennedy wanted nothing more than to stand before the nations of the world and demand that the Soviets back off or he would blast the motherfuckers off the face of the Earth. He *wanted* to, but he wouldn't because such a tenuous situation called for diplomacy. Of course, anyone who had passed eighth-grade history knew that diplomacy was the equivalent of crossing your fingers and hoping that the bully would go away. He wondered how Stu Bailey and Jeff Spencer would handle it. Knowing that the stars of the breezy, jazz-infused TV detective drama *77 Sunset Strip* would have the Soviet strongman advocating baseball and apple pie within an hour.

A few minutes before nine, the president got up and went into the living room that featured a panoramic view of the Manhattan skyline. Turned on the television, poured himself a scotch, then lit a cigar and settled into a comfortable armchair. The Secret Service detail outside his door on alert that for the next hour, he was not to be disturbed. The fate of the world could wait as the president wondered who the female guest star would be on tonight's episode of *77 Sunset Strip*. A show he never missed. A show he had once excused himself from a White House reception for the king of Sweden to watch.

True to form, Bailey and Spencer solved the case, but unfortunately, neither was able to close the deal with sexy guest star Diane McBain. The president poured himself another scotch and prepared to get back to work on his speech when, at exactly ten o'clock, one of the Secret Service agents knocked and entered.

"There are two young ladies outside in the hall who insist that we give you this card." He handed it to the president. "They have been waiting almost an hour and refuse to leave until you've read it."

"Tell them I said thank you and send them on their way."

"I think you should read the card, sir."

The president opened the envelope and brightened when he saw that the card was signed *Ring-a-ding-ding*.

"By all means" —he smiled, still in his underwear —"show the young ladies in."

A moment later, his eyes popped out of his head as he saw that they were not just young ladies. They were twins.

Blond. Statuesque. Perfect.

He poured them each a drink, his dick in attack mode as identical twins in identical threads slowly undressed each other. Fondling each other, they put on a show. He led them to the bedroom, the three of them quickly naked on the bed, where Two-Minute Jack did not last half that long. But the twins were nowhere near being finished, bringing each other to orgasm that got Jack hard again in a hurry. Took turns sucking the presidential cock as he screamed, "Ring-a-ding-ding!"

CHAPTER 22

"Thanks for the twins, Frank," Jack raved, on the phone at his desk in the Oval Office. "I don't think words exist to properly describe that rush of excitement."

"I'm glad you enjoyed them," Sinatra replied on the other end of the call.

"Did *you* enjoy them?"

"They were a special gift just for you."

"You're a pal, Frank. But do yourself a favor and spend a night with those girls. I guarantee it will change your life." The president clipped the end of a cigar and lit it with a wooden match. "And sorry I haven't been available lately, but I hope you understand it's nothing personal. This job has me by the balls nonstop, but I'm taking a little time in Hyannis Port the week after next. I know it's been way too long and we have a lot to talk about, so why don't you come up for some sailing? We can catch up and have a little fun."

"Sounds great."

"I've got to hang up, Frank. I'll call you with the details."

The president leaned back in his padded leather chair and blew a smoke ring.

"That was a mistake, Jack," said Bobby, who was seated across the desk.

"What do you have against Frank? You've never liked him."

"He's a degenerate."

"Just because a man doesn't live the squeaky-clean lifestyle you think he should, that doesn't make him a degenerate. And Frank certainly did not deserve that dirty trick you pulled on him with that phony story in the scandal magazine."

"I will continue to do whatever it takes to keep him away and protect the dignity of your presidency."

"You've got a mean streak, Bobby. Ever since you flunked the third grade."

"You can't be seen cavorting with that womanizing son of a bitch."

"*I'm* a womanizing son of a bitch," the president said.

"In private. But Sinatra shines a very public light on every one of his sordid affairs, whether it be women, gangsters, or brawling in nightclubs. Your political stock goes down whenever your name is linked to his in the press. And you know that Jackie will not stand for any sort of public humiliation, especially now with the new baby."

"Frank is my friend. Leave him alone."

"Remember what Dad always told us: It's not who you are that counts. It's who people *think* you are."

The president looked at the model of a nineteenth-century Chinese clipper displayed on the credenza beside his cigar humidor. Sailing had always been his escape, and at the moment, he would have given anything to be at the helm of his twenty-five-foot sloop, *Victura*, instead of sniping with his holier-than-thou brother.

"Frank has done a lot for me, and I would not be sitting in this chair if it weren't for him and Sam Giancana. The closest presidential race in modern American history and they swung it for me."

"Like hell they did."

"Promises were made. I owe them, Bobby."

"Those greaseballs did nothing for you. You won the election because the public believed in your integrity and your vision for the future."

"I'm sure Giancana doesn't see it that way."

"It doesn't make any difference how he sees it, because I'm going to keep squeezing that spaghetti-bender until he's locked away in prison and the Outfit is destroyed forever."

"No, you're not."

"My office—the office you appointed me to—is tasked with fighting organized crime, and for the life of me, I cannot understand why you want to cavort with a playboy like Sinatra, who brags about being close friends with Giancana, Johnny Rosselli, Mickey Cohen, and a dozen other high-profile mobsters. *And* invite him to our family home, no less. Dump him, Jack, before that Wop drags down your entire administration."

"For the last time, get it through your thick head that Frank Sinatra is my friend. And we *are* going to honor Dad's deal."

"No, Jack. We're not."

The president slammed his fist on the desk. "Don't forget you work for me, little brother."

"That's right, Jack. So let me do my job."

CHAPTER 23

"Oh, my god! Look at you!" Don Rickles exclaimed to a well-dressed woman who blushed at the compliment. "Was anybody else hurt in the accident?"

The short balding comedian sweating through his tuxedo had amassed a loyal following in a very short time, firing zingers at audiences four shows a night, six nights a week at the Casbar Theater, an intimate casino lounge inside the Sahara Hotel. And the more he insulted people, the more they loved him. Next he took aim at a young couple holding hands.

"Look, buddy, you're not in Kansas anymore. In Vegas, you don't pay the hooker to go on a date with you; you pay her for sex." He paused as the young woman held up her hand to show him her wedding ring. "Then I guess he's paying you for no sex. But seriously, how long have you lovebirds been married?"

The answer was two hours.

"Well, congratulations to you both. And I hope you'll continue to be happy for another two hours."

The bride and groom kissed, proud owners of a story to tell their grandchildren.

"And there's Frank Sinatra," Rickles called out, pointing to the king of midnight seated ringside with Dean and a collection of showgirls from Le Lido de Paris, the topless revue at the Stardust. "Frank is such a big star that when you enter the room, he makes you kiss his ring. I wouldn't mind so much, but he keeps it in his back pocket."

Rickles was building a career shooting rubber-tipped arrows at squares and celebrities alike, but some of his more famous targets took exception to being ridiculed by a rookie who had been playing lounges for less than a year, even if it was all in good fun. But not Sinatra. While it was off-limits for anyone else to poke fun at him, Sinatra loved Rickles and gave him a pass.

"And there's his pal Dean Martin, one of the greatest singers of all time. Just ask him." Rickles waited for the laughter to die down, then looked apologetically at his target. "But seriously, Dean, and I tell you this from the bottom of my heart. Nobody likes you."

The show rolled on, and after the next round of drinks were served, Sinatra told Dean that his whiskey tasted odd. That it was not Jack Daniel's.

"You're too tight to know the difference."

"I know what the real stuff tastes like better than Jack Daniel himself." Then to prove the point, Sinatra drank it down, immediately wishing he hadn't.

"This is rotgut," he yelled at the waitress. "The bartender poured from the wrong fucking bottle."

"You got a problem, Frank?" Rickles called out from the stage.

Sinatra ignored him, demanding the waitress go back to the bar to bring him the right bottle and a clean glass.

"It'll be okay, Frank," Rickles continued. "Just make yourself at home and hit somebody."

The audience grew silent as Sinatra glared at the comedian, then busted out laughing. Led the standing ovation at the end of the show, took his pick of the showgirls, and squired her back to his suite at the Sands.

It was great to be the king of midnight.

CHAPTER 24

"My dad hates Tommy," Nancy told George as they ate burgers at a sidewalk café on the Sunset Strip.

"No, he doesn't." He gave Frank's pretty daughter a reassuring smile, knowing that his boss didn't care enough about Tommy Sands to hate him. The man was a washed-up teen idol, now concentrating on acting after having had modest success with a string of pop records in the late fifties. "Mr. S. is like most fathers in that he thinks no man is good enough for his little girl."

"I'm not a little girl anymore." She had longish dark hair and was wearing jeans and a breezy yellow top. Had been close with George since he covered for her when she came home drunk once after a high school dance. "I'm a woman, but when I tell him I'm getting married, he's going to blow his top and do everything in his power to stop us. So, we're going to elope."

"Since the day you were born, Mr. S. has looked forward to dancing at your wedding. It would be selfish to deny him that."

"So, even if he gives his blessing, Dad will want my wedding to be all about him? That's reason enough to elope."

"He won't admit this even to himself but, just like most men when their first child gets married, Mr. S. will start to think of himself as old."

"My dad will never think of himself as old."

"But Tommy will be an up close and personal reminder that there is a new generation of entertainers looking to take away his spotlight."

"Tommy is no threat to him."

"Not Tommy personally, but what he represents."

"You were married once, weren't you, George?"

"Back in Louisiana."

"How come you split up? Did you fight a lot?"

"Sometimes she slept," he deadpanned. "We were happy at first, but it wasn't long before she wanted me to stop seeing my friends and spend every night at home. I couldn't see it that way."

"It won't be like that for us." Nancy beamed when she spoke of Tommy. "We love spending every minute we can together."

"And when his career stalls, then what? You can't live on love."

"That's exactly what my dad would say."

It was a sunny day, perfect for girl watching, and Nancy noticed George eying a fair mademoiselle in a short skirt seated alone.

"You know, with Dad off to Hyannis Port to see the president, you have the whole weekend to yourself." She aimed a suggestive smile across the café. "Maybe you should start it off with a little afternoon delight."

"Stop it, Nancy."

"What's the matter, George?" She smirked. "I know you're not shy."

"It's not appropriate for me to talk about sex with my boss's daughter."

"You can't stop trying to look up her skirt, can you?" Nancy teased.

George took a bite of his burger and washed it down with an icy swallow of lemonade. Then he looked at Nancy seriously. "Today you're in love, but things change. People change. How can you be sure you're going to stay in love?"

"Because there is a sincerity about Tommy. He's considerate and understanding, but Dad can't see that because he doesn't know Tommy the way I do."

"Then give Mr. S. a chance to see what a good man he is and how happy he makes you. Eventually, he'll come around."

"You really think so?"

"I know Mr. S. better than anyone, and in ways a daughter never could."

"Then you know he's going to say that I'm too young to get married."

"And your answer is to elope and deny your father the joy of walking his first-born daughter down the aisle?" He reached across the table and took her hand. "Just tell Mr. S. how you feel about Tommy, and when he sees the sparkle in your eyes, he'll know it comes from the heart and he'll give you his blessing."

"Do you really think so, George?"

"Count on it. All your father wants is for his little girl to be happy."

"Why don't you make yourself happy?" Nancy smiled as she looked across the café. "Go over and sweet-talk the girl out of that short skirt."

CHAPTER 25

"It's a thoughtful and beautiful gift," the president said as he admired the solid gold lighter that had been engraved *JACK from FRANK*. He lit a petit corona and sat back in a rocker on the porch of the Kennedy family home in Hyannis Port, Massachusetts. "And thanks for joining me for a relaxing weekend on the water. I can't even remember the last time my schedule allowed me to go sailing."

"You need to make the time."

"Easier said than done, Frank."

"You're the president."

"That's the problem." Jack looked at the presidential flag wafting in the early-evening breeze off Nantucket Sound, signifying that the chief executive was in residence. "My daily schedule is so brutal that I have zero time for myself. Even with Mother and Dad in Palm Beach, Jackie and the kids in New York, and giving the servants the weekend off, there is still no privacy with my Secret Service detail patrolling the grounds."

A bottle of Jack Daniel's and a bottle of Old Overholt on the table between them, Sinatra swirled naked ice cubes, then refilled both of their glasses.

"I didn't mean to dump this on you, Frank. It's just so goddam frustrating."

"Blow off as much steam as you need to. That's what friends are for."

"You *are* a good friend, Frank," Jack said, looking at the lighter. "And speaking of my kids, how are yours?"

Sinatra took out his wallet and showed off the latest snapshots. "Tina is in ninth grade, Frank Jr. graduated from prep school, and Nancy is becoming a woman with a mind of her own."

"Sounds like you disapprove of something."

"Don't get me wrong. Nancy is a great kid." He lit a cigarette as the sun went down for the count. "Taking classes to become an actress."

"So, what's the problem?"

"She thinks she's in love with this nobody Tommy Sands."

"Puppy love."

"She doesn't think so."

"Believe me, Frank. Nancy will forget all about this guy the first time a brighter smile catches her eye."

"So, your advice is not to worry about it? Just wait until Caroline brings home her first serious boyfriend."

"Jesus, Frank. She's only 6."

"And before you know it, she'll be 20. Enjoy your time with her while you can."

"The problem is that right now I don't have the time to enjoy anything."

"Even Jackie?"

"I adore that woman." He took a folded piece of paper from his wallet and showed it to Frank. "She wrote me this poem for our first anniversary. It's called "Meanwhile in Massachusetts," and it predicts a bright future in front of me. Those words inspire me to this day."

"Do you think she knew, even back then, that you would become president?"

"Absolutely. And she did her part to make it happen. Even pregnant with John-John, she gave interviews, taped commercials, and wrote a weekly campaign newsletter."

"Sounds like an ideal marriage."

"Jackie calls it atypical. Says that no matter what's going on in our lives and how much time we spend apart, we always find a way to show each other the love when we're together."

"Atypical? Does that mean she's okay with your other women?"

"Hell no. When you were married to Ava, was she okay with your other women?"

"I never cheated on Ava."

"What about your first wife?"

"How do you think I met Ava?"

The president took a sip of rye whiskey.

"I ordered Bobby to pull the wiretaps and stop all organized crime surveillance."

"And he agreed to that?"

"Bobby may be a self-righteous crusader hell-bent on bringing down the Outfit, but when push comes to shove, I'm the president of the United States and he'll do what I tell him. Just make Giancana understand that since Hoover and the FBI are involved, it might take a little time."

"*More* time? He's not going to like that."

"I am Bobby's boss and Bobby is Hoover's boss, so you can assure Giancana the harassment will stop." He zipped up his jacket. "On the water it always gets chilly at night."

"The nights are one of the reasons I moved to Palm Springs. The stars are so bright it makes you feel like you're in heaven," Sinatra said through a stream of cigarette smoke. "You should come out for a couple days."

"You're forgetting the president never gets a day off. And even if I was able to swing it, your phone would never stop ringing."

"I'll take it off the hook."

"What about my chaperones?" He pointed to the Secret Service agents at the end of the driveway. "I can't go anywhere without them."

"Bring them along. They can protect you from Jimmy Van Heusen's party girls."

Jack smiled, thinking back to all the spectacular women he had screwed at Wonder Palms, envying Sinatra his freedom to enjoy life to the fullest while, as president, he lived under a microscope.

"If I spent even one night at your house, not only would Jackie blow her top, but the press would have a field day."

"Not if it was an official visit."

Jack laughed at the absurdity, but Frank was serious.

"What if I built a private guest house on my property for you to use whenever you're there? It could be your presidential retreat, like Ike had at Camp David and Truman had at his Little White House in Key West. You can call it your Western White House."

"I appreciate the offer, Frank, but to spend that much time

somewhere, I would need a teletype and multiple secure phone lines."

"No problem."

"And a helipad."

"No problem."

"That's the booze talking, Frank."

"I've never been more serious in my life." Sinatra looked at the Secret Service detail patrolling the grounds. "And a bungalow for your chaperones."

Jack sat quietly for several minutes, lost in thought as he stared out at the darkness of Nantucket Sound. He placed his cigar in the ashtray and let it burn out while he finished his drink.

"Western White House, huh?"

"That's right, Mr. President."

"Establishing a base in Palm Springs would be a great political move," Jack thought out loud. "It would make me a shoo-in to carry California in '64."

"Then we're agreed?"

"Agreed. We can talk details in the morning, but right now I must attend to some presidential ring-a-ding-ding waiting for me upstairs." Jack stood and grinned. "And you might want to hurry up and empty your glass, because there are two girls waiting in your room. Not twins, but every bit as kinky."

"You're a true pal, Jack."

"And there's a phonograph, because I know you like to listen to your own records while you're in the saddle."

"You haven't missed a trick."

"Like they say, Frank, it's Sinatra's world, and the rest of us are just living in it."

Sinatra gazed out at the darkness of the Sound and saw what

Jack had seen: clarity. He was the brightest star in the showbiz galaxy enjoying a life of which mere mortals dared not even dream. And the way he saw it, now that the Outfit would soon be off his back, being Frank Sinatra was even better than being president.

He envisioned the presidential flag flying above the Western White House and how it would guarantee him a place in the history books schoolkids were forced to read but would now want to read because he had just made politics cool. He finished his drink and went inside, running face-first into Bobby Kennedy.

"Does Jack know you're here?" Sinatra demanded.

"My brother is otherwise occupied."

"And I'm about to be, so get the fuck out of my way."

"Not so fast," Bobby said, steering him into an oak-paneled study where a movie projector and screen were set up. "I want to make it clear once and for all that I am going to keep the pressure on until both Giancana and the Outfit are destroyed."

"No, you're not. Because the president of the United States, your boss, just told me he ordered you to stop the harassment and that he is going to honor the deal."

"I know what's best for Jack, and as America's chief law enforcement officer, I am bound by duty to extinguish Sam Giancana, who is not only a threat to the presidency but to every decent person in this country."

"Save the hot air. There are no reporters here."

Bobby dimmed the lights and switched on the projector. The screen filled with a frustrated Frank Sinatra trying to penetrate a gorgeous blonde with a limp dick.

"You motherfucker!" Sinatra snarled as he watched the showgirl he had taken back to his suite after the Don Rickles show attempt to arouse his cock that wanted nothing to do with her. "I knew that drink didn't taste right. There was something in it."

"Saltpeter. I arranged for the waitress to put a double dose in your Jack Daniel's." Bobby enjoyed every second as Sinatra's embarrassment rose to anger. "Maybe we should invite the two women waiting for you upstairs to come down and watch this with us."

The showgirl tickled Sinatra's balls with her tongue but got no response from a dick that drooped sadly like a wet noodle. She tried every trick she knew, and she knew them all, to get him revved up. Then, having become frustrated herself, she made the mistake of laughing and ended up on the floor with a sock in the eye.

In a rage, Sinatra ripped the reel from the projector, unwound the loose film into a waste basket, then lit it on fire.

"That was a copy, Frank. I have the original in a safe place."

"What do you want from me, you weasel?"

"Evidence I can use in court to convict Sam Giancana of a major felony. And if you don't get me that evidence, I will have copies of the film delivered to every journalist in America who has a grudge against you. You will be ridiculed mercilessly and laughed out of show business."

"I won't rat on Sam."

"The great lady-killer Frank Sinatra can't get it up with a gorgeous showgirl. Are you queer, Frank? Because that's what everyone will say."

"Nobody will believe that. I've fucked a thousand women."

"But not the one in the film. And that's all anyone will talk about."

"I won't rat on Sam," Sinatra repeated. "And even if I would, which I won't, I don't have access to any evidence you could use against him."

"I don't care if the evidence is real or planted, as long as a jury will believe it."

"There are a hundred other guys you could get to flip on Sam. So, why me?"

"Because you're an immoral degenerate who doesn't care who you hurt. So, I'm going to put a target on your back by making you roll over on Giancana, who I will then get to roll over on Marcello, Trafficante, Cohen, and every other mob boss until all the dominos fall and organized crime in America is wiped out for good."

"It will never work, little brother," Sinatra told the attorney general, the target already on his back. "You have no idea how powerful Giancana is."

"I'm giving you an ultimatum: Either get me evidence I can use against Sam Giancana or the film goes into wide distribution." Bobby was cocky and had Sinatra right where he wanted him. "Face it, Frank. One way or another, you're screwed."

"Nobody screws Frank Sinatra!"

CHAPTER 26

"This could ruin me, Mickey. I'd be laughed right out of show business."

"You say there are no close-ups and no sound on the film for a voice match, which gives us plausible deniability."

"I don't want deniability," Sinatra told his lawyer as they huddled in full crisis mode in the living room at Wonder Palms. "I want this nightmare to go away."

"Relax, Frank. We'll get you out of this."

"It's my career." Sinatra was nervous. He hadn't slept and was now pacing back and forth, George catching up to him with a drink. "It's my life."

"What I can't understand is why Bobby Kennedy would blackmail you. What does he want?"

"Evidence that will put Sam Giancana in prison."

"My God, Frank. What the hell have you gotten yourself into?" Even though it was not yet noon, Mickey felt the need for a bracer and asked George to bring him some vodka with a splash of grapefruit juice. "I need to know everything, so start from the beginning."

Sinatra sat down across the coffee table, his orange mohair sweater melting into the orange sofa. Then, in great detail, he told his attorney about the deal Joe Kennedy had proposed in that very room, wanting Giancana to fix the election in exchange for Jack putting an end to the organized crime surveillance. How Jack was attempting to honor the deal but Bobby continued to ramp up the pressure behind Jack's back, figuring if he could bust Giancana, he could get the mobster to roll over on the rest of the Outfit bosses, thereby ridding America of organized crime and making himself a lock for the White House in '68.

"It's a plan that won't work unless he first gets Giancana," said Mickey, connecting the dots. "And to get Giancana, Bobby needs evidence that you possess."

"That's just it. I don't know anything that would put the finger on Sam and wouldn't rat him out even if I did. But if I don't do something, he's going to send copies of that fucking film to absolutely everyone."

"Have you told Giancana about this?"

"You think I'm fucking crazy? He already blames me for the Kennedys not honoring the deal."

"I thought the two of you were close."

"Sam is like a brother. But he's also a killer, and I've seen him turn on a dime."

Mickey Rudin had nefarious connections of his own he had used as fixers, saving the careers of some of Hollywood's biggest stars, including an Oscar-winning chicken fucker and a snatch-happy Grace Kelly, each time making every bit of proof disappear without one word of gossip or press coverage. And he would rescue Sinatra as well, though, as it always seemed to be with Frank, the stakes were considerably higher.

"This isn't a typical shakedown where I can arrange to have the evidence stolen or scare the blackmailer within an inch of his life."

"It's still blackmail," Sinatra ranted. "Can't we have the son of a bitch arrested?"

"Rule number one when trying to keep a lid on something is to never involve the police. Especially this time because Bobby Kennedy is the attorney general of the United States, which, for all intents and purposes, places him above the law. Besides, at this point, it's just your word against his." Mickey sipped his drink, taking a moment to consider what they were up against. "Maybe our best move is to get out in front of this. Go on the offensive and control the narrative before he can by spreading the word that someone is threatening to blackmail you with a doctored film. That it's a phony."

"It *is* a fucking phony! He drugged me and staged the whole goddam thing!"

"The only leverage Bobby Kennedy has is that you are terrified of the film going public. But if we go public with our version of the story first, he will have nothing to gain by releasing it."

"Except spite. That son of a bitch hates my guts. Says I'm an immoral degenerate."

"We have the best publicists in the business who can spin the story in such a way that even your worst enemies would believe the film to be a phony."

"It *is* a fucking phony!"

"But to make our narrative iron-clad believable, we would need someone to corroborate the story. Maybe pay the girl to say that it's not you in the film with her."

"I gave her a black eye."

"Then pay her a lot."

"I don't like it." Sinatra put out one cigarette, then lit another. "You can't trust a broad not to crack under pressure, which, if she did, would confirm the bullshit that I have a limp dick. Or even worse, that I'm a queer."

"What does the president say about all this?"

"He's grateful to me and to Sam for putting him in the White House, and he promised to order Bobby to back off."

"The blackmail or the Outfit surveillance?"

"Both."

"Then what's the problem?"

"Bobby won't do it. No matter what Jack orders him to do, that fucking weasel says he is bound by duty to protect the president's image by keeping me away from him, while at the same time ridding the country of organized crime. The son of a bitch is drunk with power."

"What are the odds that the president will take your side against his own brother?"

Sinatra told him about the Western White House and took him outside to show him where Jack's guest house would be built as well as the Secret Service bungalow and the communications room. All off to one side of the property to preserve the view of the golf course from the main house.

"Jack would never have given me the okay to start construction unless he had my back."

"But for how long? Because when push comes to shove, blood trumps friendship every day of the week."

"Not this time."

"Are you willing to bet your career on that?"

"*Maybe* getting out in front of this by going public is the best way to handle it. *Maybe* blood does trump friendship. But there are too many goddam maybes, and I can't take the chance of sitting around like a schmuck waiting for the world to come crashing down on my fucking head." Sinatra picked up a chair and angrily threw it into the pool. "I want a *guarantee* that this problem is going to go away."

"Then get something on Bobby Kennedy and put *him* on the defensive."

CHAPTER 27

"How the hell am I supposed to get something on that weasel to put him on the defensive? He's a fucking Boy Scout," Sinatra griped. Insomnia and frustration eating away at him as he and George had morning coffee by the pool. "Sam used to have his house and office bugged, and all he found out was that the prick almost never drinks and doesn't cheat on his wife, that he gets his rocks off collecting stamps."

"Does Mr. Sam still have those tapes? Because you could splice bits together and make it sound like Bobby said something incriminating."

Over the years Frank had come to consider George a friend who, as witness to most of the intimate comings and goings of his life, had proven he could be trusted with any secret. He valued George's opinion, as it was often more pragmatic than his own, but this time, his valet had hit a foul ball.

"We couldn't do it without involving Sam." He looked out at the golfers on the seventeenth fairway, at this moment envying the squares whose biggest concern was where to eat lunch. "The Outfit bosses are pissed off enough as it is, so I'm not about to make things worse by telling him there is even more trouble in Camelot."

"Bobby can't possibly be as clean as you think he is. He must have a skeleton buried somewhere in his closet."

"It must be buried deep because, by all accounts, he's the most boring son of a bitch who ever drew breath."

Frustrated. Discouraged. Back to square one.

The telephone rang.

"Good morning, Mr. President," George said after answering.

"Jack, goddam it," came the voice on the other end. "I told you to call me Jack."

"One moment. Mr. S. is right here."

"How are things in Washington?" Sinatra greeted in his cheeriest voice, hoping for the best but fearing the worst.

"Raining like hell," the president told him. "But I have good news for you. I got the film from Bobby and destroyed it."

And just like that, Frank Sinatra's worst nightmare was over. He smiled and gave George a thumbs-up. No need for publicists or to put the weasel on the defensive. One telephone call and it was all over.

"So, tell me, Frank. How is progress coming on my presidential retreat?"

"The architect is working on the plans, and the contractor is pulling permits. He says he should be able to start work in a few weeks."

"I can't wait. How's the weather out there?"

"Absolutely gorgeous day," he said as he looked out at another foursome on the fairway, pitying the squares with their small lives who dared not even dream of how amazing it was to be Frank Sinatra.

But George wasn't completely sold, thinking back to when the president had sucker-punched Sammy Davis Jr. three days before the inauguration. The Kennedys were users. Joe, Bobby, and even though the jury was still out on Jack, George knew that Mickey Rudin was right when he said that blood trumped friendship every day of the week. That even though his boss was, at least for the moment, enjoying a victory, nothing had changed as the threat of Outfit retaliation for failing to stop the continued FBI surveillance was still hanging over Sinatra's head.

CHAPTER 28

"More fucking time?" griped Trafficante. "How much more time, Sam? This jagoff has been feeding us the same line so long it seems like forever."

"Yeah, Sam. Enough is enough," added a pissed-off Marcello, spitting on the seat in front of him. "The Feds got so many bugs planted I can't even take a shit without Bobby Kennedy hearing me flush."

Playing afternoon hooky to cheer on the Cubs was a Chicago tradition, even though they could always be counted upon to find new ways of losing a baseball game. Which was why an empty section of the upper deck at Wrigley Field was available for the three gangsters to speak privately.

"It's that fucking Sinatra," Marcello said. "His friend the president fucked us over, and he has to make it right."

"It's obvious after all this time he doesn't have the influence he said he had," Trafficante groused. "Nothing but lip service while we keep taking it up the ass."

"Let me feed him to the gators."

"For chrissakes, Carlos," Giancana barked. "Will you shut up about the fucking alligators?"

"Then maybe a visit to that pretty daughter of his will shake him up enough to make things right," Marcello continued to rant.

"No one touches Frank's family," Giancana said. "You know goddam well that the Outfit never goes after anyone's family except as a last resort."

"Then if Sinatra doesn't make this right, Sam, and soon, we have to cut our losses and disappear him, just like we would any other welsher."

"Not yet." Giancana raised his voice to be heard over the crowd coming to life as the Cubs loaded the bases.

"Why have you let him get away with this bullshit for so goddam long?" Trafficante demanded to know. "Do you have something going on that we don't know about?"

Strike three. Inning over.

"Sinatra makes a hundred grand a week singing songs in Vegas while our business is in the shitter. Even though it's peanuts compared to what we're losing, that money should go to us," Trafficante reasoned.

"He's right, Sam," Marcello added. "He pays or he's dead."

"Nobody touches Frank Sinatra!" Giancana yelled. "Not yet."

CHAPTER 29

Villa Venice was a run-of-the-mill spaghetti joint just outside Chicago in suburban Wheeling until Sam Giancana—behind a respectable front man—upgraded it to an elegant supper club and showroom that seated eight hundred. A block away from a roadway maintenance depot hidden from traffic by bulldozers and other heavy construction equipment that the gangster had transformed into a plush gambling casino. Using Frank Sinatra as a shill to lure high rollers who, after shows at the Villa Venice, would blow their bankrolls at the dice tables.

Sinatra did not disappoint the sold-out opening night audience that included Trafficante, Marcello, and a who's who of the underworld seated ringside—pissed-off gangsters who now understood why Giancana was protecting Sinatra. Even with a steep cover charge and overpriced drinks, men in tuxedos escorting women in mink stoles were willing to fork over top dollar to watch from the bar. A small fortune that was peanuts compared to the action at the makeshift casino where Giancana would rake in millions during Sinatra's two-week engagement, money he would not share with Trafficante,

Marcello, and the other bosses. But since Giancana was the boss of all bosses, they sucked it up and kept their mouths shut. For now.

Sinatra wowed the packed house with hits including "One for My Baby" and "Fly Me to the Moon" as well as some of his favorite B-sides. He was performing at the Villa Venice for free, knowing that the gesture would keep him safe until the surveillance finally stopped. Though, as an excellent businessman, he recorded the opening night show for a live album to be released on his Reprise label, which he figured would net him half a million.

After two encores, Frank and Sam had a drink alone in the upstairs dressing room, smiling at the result of their efforts as they looked through one-way glass at the delighted crowd that continued to live it up as the orchestra segued into dance music. And even though Giancana was as happy as Frank had seen him in a long time, he was not surprised when the conversation took a serious turn.

"You told me the FBI surveillance was being pulled, but I still have cheap suits following me everywhere."

"I also told you Jack said that because Hoover was involved it would take just a little more time."

"Meanwhile you're building that prick a fancy vacation home."

"Look, Sam," Frank said as he lit a Chesterfield, his eyes squinting against the smoke. "I can only tell you what Jack tells me."

"I would feel a lot more confident if he would tell *me*."

"Construction on the Western White House is almost complete, and Jack is coming out for a visit in three weeks. Why don't you come, too, and then we can all sit down over a drink and work this whole thing out once and for all."

CHAPTER 30

Jacqueline Kennedy projected the epitome of elegance and sophistication. The perfect wife and mother, with hardly a week passing without her photo gracing the cover of magazines such as *Look, Time,* and *Ladies' Home Journal.* She was embraced by an America tired of accepting first ladies who looked like old stoves—Mamie Eisenhower, Bess Truman, and that fugitive from a monster movie Eleanor Roosevelt. And just as she had introduced the image of a modern first lady, she was in the midst of doing the same with a long-neglected White House that had not been fully renovated since before the Civil War.

Mrs. Kennedy pushed Congress to enact legislation declaring the White House a museum and embarked on a project that remained true to historical integrity by locating and acquiring the finest furniture and artifacts dating back to 1800, when the residence was first occupied by President John Adams. She worked tirelessly with experts on American antiquities and the decorative arts on the huge undertaking, which she preferred to call preservation rather than mere restoration, that was scheduled to be celebrated with a television special later in the year when the work was complete. She brought culture to the White House, as evidenced by a portable stage set up in the East Room where later that evening cellist Pablo Casals would perform for a gathering of Nobel laureates.

It had been a long day for the first lady. *But aren't they all?* Jackie thought as she made her way from a meeting with decorators back to the Executive Residence to relax and change before the performance. Stopped as she heard noises coming from inside the Lincoln bedroom and opened the door to discover Marilyn Monroe riding reverse cowgirl on top of her husband.

Jack was scared shitless.

Marilyn smiled and held out her hand.

"Not this time, tramp."

Marilyn got dressed double quick and scrammed the hell out of there.

"I told you what I would do if I ever caught you with her again."

From her purse Jackie took the razor-sharp stiletto she always carried, a knife that had been given to her by her father after she had been annoyed by a group of boys the summer after her freshman year at Vassar.

"You wouldn't dare," he said, protecting himself with a lace pillow.

"Look into my eyes, Jack." She stepped closer.

"Please, Jackie! I promise I'll never do it again."

"You won't be able to."

He scrambled off the bed, but she blocked his path to the door and slashed the pillow.

"Don't, Jackie! Please!"

She looked at the leader of the free world crying like a baby as he stood there naked, pleading for another chance.

"Another chance to humiliate me? In my own home?"

"I'm sorry, Jackie. I swear I will never do it again. Just give me the chance to prove it."

"No."

"Please, Jackie! I'm begging you!"

"But I will give you a choice: castration, or learn the name of my girlfriend the year I studied in Paris."

"I don't know what kind of trick you're playing, Jackie, but I choose the name. Put down the knife and tell me her name."

"Only if you promise never to see Marilyn again."

"I promise."

"Or any other slut."

"I promise. Now put down the knife."

"Not until you also promise that you will never set foot inside that whorehouse Frank Sinatra is building for you in Palm Springs."

"Frank has spent a fortune on construction."

The epitome of elegance and sophistication grabbed her husband's cock, pulled it taut and held the blade beneath it.

"Jackie, please! Don't do this!"

Drops of blood fell onto the carpet as the sharp blade nicked his flesh.

"Okay! Okay!" he sobbed. "I'll never see Frank again. Now put down the knife and tell me the girl's name."

"Her name was Caroline."

The remaining color drained from his face.

"She pronounced it Caroleen. So sexy the way she said it, and for a year, I was in love with her."

"Stop it, Jackie."

"It made you sick watching Caroline's mother having sex with your movie star whore in Las Vegas. And now every time you hear your daughter's name, every time you look at her, you will think of me doing the same thing with Carol*een*." Jackie again grabbed her husband's cock and held the sharp blade against it. "And if I ever hear even a rumor about you seeing Sinatra, I'll feed your dick to the dog."

CHAPTER 31

Back home after his two-week run at the Villa Venice, Sinatra was more than pleased as he inspected the newly completed Western White House. The living room had a white brick fireplace, shag carpeting, and contemporary furniture with orange accent pieces. Off the living room was an office with a teletype and multiple phone lines, as Jack had requested. The master bedroom had a sauna and walk-in closet. There was an ultra-modern kitchen that George would stock with all the president's favorites, and a bar already stocked with 100-proof Old Overholt and all Jack's other preferred intoxicants. There was a cigar humidor filled with H. Upmann petit coronas, and succulents and cacti added exterior desert accents. The cement for the helipad was scheduled to be poured in the morning. Every last detail was perfect for his best pal, who would arrive in a week. Six days, actually, not that Frank was counting.

To legitimize his booze-and-broads holiday, Jack was scheduled to visit with former President Eisenhower, tour the Welwood Murray Memorial Library, and answer a few softball questions at a Riviera Hotel media event organized by the White House press secretary,

Pierre Salinger. Then Jack would settle in at Wonder Palms for a very private meeting with Sam Giancana that would once and for all put an end to the organized crime surveillance and—most importantly for Sinatra—get him off the hook with the Outfit bosses who held him accountable.

Even for the brightest star in the showbiz galaxy, life had never been this exciting. The only downer being that Nancy had ambushed him with news that she was planning to marry Tommy Sands, who Frank saw as an opportunist looking to revive his career by marrying a Sinatra. His ex-wife Nancy, whom they had named their daughter after, was all for the marriage, which was just another reason for Frank to oppose it, but he loved his daughter so much that there was nothing he could do but take the high road and hope for the best.

He made a few calls, then caught forty winks by the pool. Make that twenty as Lawford, always dressed to the nines even on a warm desert afternoon, walked out to join him.

"Hello, Charlie. Even you couldn't spoil this beautiful day," Frank beamed, then dimmed the wattage as he saw the uneasy look on Lawford's face. "But you're going to try, aren't you?"

"Don't shoot the messenger, Frank."

"Spit it out."

"Jack isn't coming."

"The trip has been postponed?"

"He's still coming to Palm Springs." Lawford gulped, mustering his resolve. "He's just not staying here."

Sinatra bolted off the chaise lounge and pointed toward the presidential guest house. "I built that *for Jack*. To *his* specifications. And you're telling me he's not going to fucking stay in it?"

"I'm sorry, Frank."

"Then where the hell is he staying?"

"At Bing Crosby's."

"Crosby's!" Sinatra exploded.

Crosby was his friend. Crosby had once been his mentor. Crosby was a fucking Republican!

"Calm down, Frank."

"Don't tell me to calm down, you fucking errand boy. That weasel Bobby is behind this."

"It's not Bobby."

"If you lie to me one more time, I'll knock your ass into the pool."

"It's Jackie. She caught him with Marilyn."

"So what? She's his wife, not his warden."

"I don't know what she threatened him with, but Jack is scared to death of her. That's why he sent me here to talk to you, hoping you would understand."

Sinatra slugged him so hard he stumbled backward and splashed into the pool. "I warned you not to lie to me, errand boy."

Lawford climbed out of the water, his silk suit drenched.

"Jack did not send you here." Sinatra glared at him. "It was the weasel."

"It was Jack."

"Jack would never do that."

"His exact words were, 'Tell Frank we had a lot of fun, but the president can't afford to be linked to a man who publicly associates with gangsters.'"

"Can the president afford to have a brother-in-law who likes it whips-and-chains kinky with colored streetwalkers?"

"Jack said never to contact him again."

Sinatra could see by the look on Lawford's face that he was telling the truth, but that did not stop him from slugging him again. This time into the deep end.

"You're an ingrate, Frank," Lawford yelled as he treaded water.

"And you're a fucking parasite."

"You would never have met Jack if it weren't for me."

"The Kennedys think you're a joke, and they'll kick your ass to the curb when they have no more use for you." Sinatra was raging. "You can consider yourself uninvited from Nancy's wedding on Saturday, and you're fired from the Rat Pack show. I don't know why I hired your sorry ass in the first place. You can't sing or dance worth a shit, and I'd be better off replacing you with a cigar store Indian."

"You're nothing but a bully from the wrong side of the tracks."

"Get out of my pool, and get the fuck off my property!" Sinatra yelled. "And not through the house. Haul your waterlogged carcass over the fence and don't ever come back!"

George set a drink on the table. It went untouched for hours as Sinatra sat quietly, thinking about how simple his life had always been. He ate when he was hungry. Fucked when he was horny. Punched someone when he was pissed off. Then he overreached and lost control. About to be humiliated because he had made such a big noise in the press about his Western White House. And to top it all off, he'd been blown off by an errand boy because Jack didn't have the balls to tell him to his face.

After the sun had set, Sinatra went into the garage and grabbed a can of gasoline and an ax, then he went outside and chopped down the presidential flagpole. Doused John F. Kennedy's custom-built guest house in gasoline and struck a match. Pulled up two chairs and asked George to bring a bottle and glasses.

The men watched the guest house burn.

"So, George, has the president proven to be your hope for the future?"

"All this time in office, and he's still a disappointment, Mr. S." George emptied his drink and poured another. "It's obvious that if there is ever to be racial equality in this country, it will have to happen through activism and protests. Because there will never be anything other than lip service from the Oval Office, no matter who is sitting behind the desk."

Sirens blared as they raced up Wonder Palms Road, and the two friends sipped their drinks as firemen rushed hoses past them, quickly getting the blaze under control.

In Sinatra's world, a man's word was his bond and a man stood by his friends. But it had finally become obvious that Jack Kennedy had never been his friend and had used him from the start. A politician saying what Frank wanted to hear in order to get what he wanted. That he never had any intention to end the organized crime surveillance, and once it hit the papers that the president was jilting him to stay with Bing Crosby, Giancana would be through protecting him from Marcello and the other bosses who held him responsible for everything.

Meaning that unless he could come up with a way to stop Bobby Kennedy's vendetta against the Outfit—and fast—Frank Sinatra was a dead man.

CHAPTER 32

"What's eating you, pally?" Dean asked as he and Frank had a drink at the casino bar outside the Copa Room at the Sands. "It's the bride who's supposed to be nervous."

But Sinatra's uneasiness had nothing to do with his first-born daughter marrying Tommy Sands in a few minutes. He steered the conversation to Dean's early days in Steubenville.

"What are you getting at?" Dean wanted to know as he straightened the carnation pinned to the lapel of Sinatra's dark-blue suit. "In all the years I've known you, you've never once asked me about what went on there."

Gambling, prostitution, and murder. Those were the main industries of the small eastern Ohio town when Dean, born Dino Crocetti, had packed his bags in search of the big time.

"You must have known a lot of guys—not connected guys— who would do anything if the price was right."

"Half the yobbos I used to deal cards to at the Spot would murder their own mothers for a carton of cigarettes."

"You still in touch with any of them?"

"Whatever you have in mind, it's a bad idea."

"Get me a phone number, Dean."

"Don't be stupid, Frank."

"Get me a number, Dean."

"Excuse me, Frank," casino boss Jack Entratter interrupted. "They're ready to start the ceremony."

"We'll be there in a minute."

"Creating that beautiful young woman who's about to be married is the best thing you ever did," Dean said with a smile, sliding off his barstool as Entratter walked away into the Copa Room. "So, do yourself a favor and put whatever is troubling you in the rearview mirror and go back to enjoying life as Frank Sinatra."

Sinatra took a final drag, then crushed out his Chesterfield, wishing Giancana could be there, as weddings strengthened the bonds of friendship, even if just for the moment. A moment he could have used as a last chance to try to square things and get himself off the hook before it was too late. But due to the mobster's name on the Gaming Control Board's List of Excluded Persons he could not set foot inside the Sands without being arrested. Maybe it was already too late to make things right, but Giancana coming to Vegas in the morning made it tomorrow's worry.

Frank pulled George close and gave him a hug, and then they walked into the showroom Sinatra had made famous.

The bride was a vision in a traditional white lace gown, her dark hair curled perfectly into place.

Tommy Sands was a nobody on the fast track to becoming a never-was. But Nancy was Frank Sinatra's little girl, and when he walked her down the aisle, there was a tear in his eye.

CHAPTER 33

"Bring me a fucking fork," Giancana yelled at the waiter in the empty Chinese restaurant, then slammed down his chopsticks and glared across the table at Sinatra. "How the hell can you make things right when you can't even get Jack to stay in a house you built for him?"

"Money. I can make good the loss."

"To every boss? In your dreams, you'll never have that kind of money. And even if you did, it wouldn't stop the FBI surveillance."

"Then Bobby Kennedy has to go."

"Stop talking like a gangster. You're not a fucking gangster!" Giancana yelled. "And I am *not* killing Bobby Kennedy. After staring down Khrushchev during the missile crisis, the president has never been more popular. And the weasel is riding on his brother's coattails, which makes him untouchable."

"Then I'll find another way."

"The president gave you the air. It's over."

Sinatra noticed that Giancana was not wearing the sapphire ring he had given him, and all of a sudden, the man who had never been afraid of anything in his life knew the true feeling of fear.

"I could ..."

"No more talk." Giancana got up and tossed some money on the table. "We're going for a ride."

As the black Eldorado rolled toward downtown, Frank thought about Nancy on her honeymoon and hoped that Tommy Sands would prove to be a good man who would protect her and make her happy. Thought about how Tina and Frank Jr. would have to go the rest of the way without him. Thought about how it had all started with twenty thousand bobbysoxers skipping school to storm Broadway's Paramount Theater, leading to a montage of career highlights too numerous to remember until helping elect a president proved to be his undoing. The king of midnight. The king of showbiz. The king of motherfucking everything. Yet, he was being taken for a ride—an Oscar-winning actor reduced to a tired movie cliché.

The car stopped in front of a shuttered auto repair shop on Commerce Street, and Sinatra was prodded inside by the gangster he had regarded as a brother. To the back of the garage against a rack of old tires. The end of the line.

He saw George.

"What are you doing here?"

"Mr. Sam called and said ..."

Giancana put a bullet in George's head.

Sinatra was horrified as his friend's body dropped to the oil-stained floor.

"Get on your knees and take a good look."

It was all Sinatra could do to keep from throwing up, pressed inches away from a ring of blood spatter surrounding the crater where George's eye used to be.

"You have one week to make things right, Frank."

He tried to get up, but Giancana grabbed his shoulder and held him down.

"Take a *good* look, so you understand that seven days doesn't mean eight."

CHAPTER 34

Sinatra walked through an underground passageway, past a boiler room, laundry, and catering kitchen to the service elevator. A left-handed means of entry to the Carlyle Hotel he had last used years earlier with wife Ava Gardner to avoid a crush of photographers outside the lobby. He pressed the button for the twenty-sixth floor, but the car wouldn't move without an access key, so he pressed twenty-five and rode upward. Got off and looked around. Then down to twenty-four where he smiled at a woman in a neatly pressed uniform coming out of one of the guest rooms.

"Good evening, Mr. Sinatra," said the maid, a rather plain woman a bit past her prime. "Is there something I can help you with?"

"Do you have access to the twenty-sixth floor?"

She showed him a key on her ring that would unlock the Presidential Suite.

"I left my wallet by the piano last night. I know Jack isn't in right now, but if you would be so kind as to take me upstairs to get it, I would really appreciate it."

"You should come back when the president returns."

"Normally, I would. But I'm on my way to see *A Thousand Clowns* at the O'Neill Theatre, and the tickets are in the wallet."

On a steady diet of presidents, kings, and movie stars, the staff at the Carlyle were rarely starstruck, but when Sinatra turned on the charm, this Plain Jane never stood a chance, and a moment later, they were on the elevator. Off on twenty-six. Past hand-carved Art Deco murals and into the living room of the Presidential Suite.

"I don't see your wallet," she said as she checked around the piano. "The regular housekeeper must have taken it to the lost and found."

"Or more than likely Jack put it somewhere safe. I'll just wait for him."

Which had been Sinatra's plan all along, to get inside the suite without being stopped by the president's security detail while Jack was giving a speech across town.

"I'm sorry, Mr. Sinatra, but I can't leave you here alone."

They heard a key in the lock, then both ducked down the hall as a Secret Service agent entered.

"I could get fired if he tells my supervisor that I brought you up here," the nervous woman said quietly.

"Take a breath," Frank whispered. "Now, walk out like you are supposed to be here and tell him that you brought up fresh towels."

That is exactly what the maid told the Secret Service agent, who performed only a cursory check of the suite while Sinatra stayed out of sight until he heard them both leave, then made himself comfortable in the living room and waited. Pondering the jam he was in, he believed that, no matter what had previously transpired between them, when he explained face-to-face that he was behind the eight ball, Jack would not let him down.

But what if Jack didn't come back right after his speech? Frank had no idea when he would be returning but would wait all night if necessary. Poured himself a drink and watched the sun set across the Hudson River.

"How the hell did you get in here?" snapped the president as he walked in on Sinatra making himself at home. "Didn't Peter tell you never to contact me again?"

"I needed to hear it from you."

"I'm in a hurry," Jack said as he went into the master bedroom and put on a clean shirt. "I have to change for dinner with Governor Rockefeller."

"I only need a minute of your time. It's important."

"Hand me my cufflinks."

Sinatra did.

"Not those. Get me the gold ones on the dresser."

Sinatra did.

"Look, Jack. I'm on the spot. I don't want to sound overly dramatic, but if the organized crime surveillance doesn't stop in the next six days, Giancana is going to have me killed."

"You *are* being overly dramatic."

"Dammit, Jack. We got you elected, and the bill for that is more than two years past due."

"I don't know what you're talking about."

"You made promises."

"My *father* made promises."

"You sat by my pool and told me to tell Sam not to worry, that you would honor the deal and call off the FBI surveillance. You told me the same thing at Hyannis Port, but instead, you turned your back while Bobby cranked up the heat. And the Outfit blames me because I brokered the deal."

"I can't help you, Frank."

"You're the only person who *can* help me."

Jack gargled Listerine and spit it into the bathroom sink.

"Bobby finally convinced me that, to protect my presidency, I have to distance myself from you because of your association with criminals."

"Your weasel brother is the fucking criminal. Or have you forgotten that he set me up and tried to blackmail me?"

Jack laughed.

"You think that's funny?"

"I've seen the film."

"You said you destroyed it."

"You never know when something that valuable might come in handy." Jack laughed again. "In fact, I watched it again recently with Peter. What a hoot. The great lover who can't get it up."

"At least the broads don't call me Two-Minute Jack."

"Hand me my hairbrush."

"Dammit, Jack. I wouldn't be here if I wasn't really up against it."

"I told you no."

Sinatra looked at the man preening in front of the mirror. "You were never my friend. It's just like George said. You're nothing by a user."

"How is George?"

"Giancana put a bullet in his head, and I'm next if you don't help me."

"You got yourself into this mess, Frank. You're on your own."

"You're a fucking asshole," Sinatra yelled as his frustration reached its limit. "You used me from the start. You probably even arranged the chance meeting where Lawford introduced us because I would be good for your campaign."

"It got me elected."

"And now it's going to get *me* killed."

"Is everything all right, Mr. President?" asked one of two Secret Service agents who had heard raised voices and entered the suite. "We were unaware you had a guest."

"Escort Mr. Sinatra downstairs and out of the hotel." Then the president turned to Frank. "Don't try to come back. Here or anywhere else. Because if you ever try to contact me again, I will make sure the world sees that film."

CHAPTER 35

After striking out at the Carlyle, then arranging to have George's body shipped to his parents in Louisiana, Sinatra was in no mood to be back in Vegas for a black-tie fundraiser. All he wanted to do was to hole up in the solitude of Wonder Palms and figure how to get out of an impossible jam. But Jack Entratter had established an orphans' home in Israel to honor his recently deceased wife, and the boss man of the Sands was counting on Frank's presence to goose donations.

Dean and Smokey were there as well, along with a who's who of Strip headliners, and lots of pretty girls. Entratter was never one to host stuffy events. He threw *parties*. And he was pulling out all the stops with this one, as evidenced by the entrance of two futuristic beauties with sparkling asymmetrical hair who looked as if they had arrived by spaceship.

Fashion was beginning to change in a big way as the emerging sixties hipster set began to declare independence from the jet set. You couldn't see it yet in Miami, Chicago, or even Vegas, but in London and New York, hemlines were rising. Eye-popping colors and bold, disproportionate shapes turned heads as fashion-forward women became the centerpiece of a new, younger glitterati that had no time for the middle-aged singers their parents listened to. They read *Playboy* for the articles, listened to rock and roll, and turned their backs on social convention. Yet, for some reason, one of the interstellar cuties set her sights on Sinatra. Maybe it was because he was the biggest star in the room, or maybe she just wanted to make her former bobby-soxer mother jealous, but whatever the reason, the stunner in the shimmering electric-pink minidress and matching boots was all over him.

Women in evening gowns got a close-up look at the generation that would soon put them out to pasture while their husbands handicapped how long it would take Sinatra to close the deal. But Frank wanted no part of her. Any other night he would have screwed the sexy dish on the stage just to show the Vegas A-listers that he could, but right now all he wanted was a good night's sleep before heading home to Palm Springs to figure a way out of the corner he was in.

"Send her my way when you're done," Dean smiled.

"She's all yours. I don't want her."

"What's the matter, pally? You turning queer?"

The word *queer* triggered the president's threat to make the blackmail film public, and Sinatra changed his mind, figuring it would enhance his reputation as a lady-killer to be seen leaving with the jaw-dropping beauty. He said all the necessary good nights, then made a big show of escorting her from the ballroom.

Her hand down his pants in the elevator. Her dress on the floor the moment they entered his suite. Both quickly naked as his erection guided them into the bedroom, where she screamed as they faced two hard-looking men with guns.

"Sam said I had a week," Sinatra protested.

"Shut up."

One of the gunmen grabbed the girl by the hair, dragged her through the suite, and pushed her, naked, into the hall. Threw her clothes out after her, then slammed the door.

"Call Sam!" Sinatra put up a brave front for a naked man facing a gun, but he was scared shitless. "He gave me a week!"

"I said shut up!" one of the gunmen yelled as he smashed Sinatra against the wall.

The other restrained him with handcuffs.

"You're under arrest."

CHAPTER 36

Sinatra was surrounded by cement block walls—a sink with no mirror, a narrow cot and a toilet bowl inches from his pillow. He wore baggy dungarees with no belt, a sweatshirt, and canvas slippers. His only human contact was the guards who brought him runny oatmeal for breakfast, stale cheese sandwiches for lunch, and beans for dinner. Food was the only way Sinatra could tell the time of day or how many days had passed since he had been locked inside the tiny windowless cell. He couldn't sleep. Just lay in the dark on the hard cot, his neck and back stiff.

He struggled to keep his mind from unraveling, as he had nothing to do but think the same thoughts over and over again. Freedom. Revenge. The Kennedys, Giancana, and George Jacobs. Freedom. Revenge. His home and his kids. Freedom. Revenge. Revenge. His anger festered as he waited for his captor to show his face. He wanted a cigarette.

On the fifth day, his captor finally showed his face.

"A well-known Commie sympathizer, right where you belong," said Bobby Kennedy, who stood in the doorway of the six-by-nine-foot jail cell.

"That's a fucking lie!" Sinatra yelled, spitting the words as he stood face-to-face with the man who had imprisoned him.

"A Commie who is about to be charged with treason."

"You'll never get away with it."

"What do you hear from your Commie pal Nikita Khrushchev? When he was in the U.S. in 1959, you were the emcee at a luncheon in his honor."

"Hosted by Twentieth Century Fox! Every star in Hollywood was there: Bob Hope, Cary Grant, Liz Taylor. Everybody!"

"But everybody didn't offer to take the Soviet premier on a personal guided tour of Disneyland."

"American hospitality for a visiting head of state."

"*Communist* head of state. In the middle of a nuclear arms race, you invited America's most dangerous enemy to go see Mickey Mouse."

"We never went because his security detail wouldn't allow it."

"All that matters is how all of this will sound to a jury."

"I invited him to fucking Disneyland. That's not a crime."

"You have an answer for everything, don't you?" The attorney general stepped closer. Sinatra stumbled backward until he fell onto the toilet. "But what happens when the FBI finds classified government documents in your home?"

"They won't find any classified documents in my home unless you planted them there."

"Treason is the most serious charge there is. More serious than murder."

Sinatra got off the toilet but was still trapped in the corner of the cramped cell.

"You'll never make it stick."

"Not many people know the names of Revolutionary War heroes like Henry Knox and John Stark, but every person in America despises Benedict Arnold. And just like Arnold, you will be branded a traitor. You will be locked inside a maximum-security prison for the rest of your life. You'll be a disgrace to your children, their lives ruined forever." Bobby took a step back and tempered his tone. "But it doesn't have to be that way. All you have to do is get me the evidence I need to convict Sam Giancana of a major felony."

"All the Outfit bosses blame me for your fucking FBI surveillance, and right now I couldn't get anywhere near Sam without taking a bullet in the head."

"The Outfit is a snake trying to strangle the country. And everyone knows that the only way to kill a snake is to cut off its head. Which is what I will do when you give up Giancana, putting an end to organized crime in America."

"What I've never understood is why you went after Sam and the other Outfit guys in the first place, considering your old man used to be one of them."

"My father was never a gangster. He was a businessman who made his fortune on Wall Street."

"Insider trading."

"Which was legal then."

"How about during Prohibition when he ran booze with the same guys you are trying to send to prison now? You're nothing but a hypocritical little weasel trying to make a name for yourself by biting the hand that put a silver spoon in your mouth."

"My father made an honest living during a difficult time."

"Your father was a fucking criminal. And the only reason you have your job, Mr. Attorney General, is because that welsher made a deal with Sam Giancana that got your brother elected—the same Sam Giancana you want me to help you put in prison. You're a piece of shit. The only thing I don't understand is why you're going after me. You've had a hard-on for me since before Jack announced he was running, and I want to know why. And don't give me any more of that bullshit about me being an immoral degenerate."

"Colleen Duffy."

"Who the hell is that?" Sinatra asked.

"A 17-year-old high school student who worked for my family as a part-time maid and sang in the church choir on Sundays. She was naive and innocent until you forced your attentions on her."

"That never happened."

"Later, when she discovered she was with child, she couldn't stand the shame and jumped off the Sagamore Bridge."

"I'm telling you, it wasn't me. I don't know what the hell you're talking about."

"Are you denying you were at my family's Memorial Day picnic at Hyannis Port four years ago? A party of sailing, barbeque, and touch football."

"Yeah, I was there. But I never laid a finger on any high school girl because I was busy putting the moves on your sister Pat."

"Your friend Peter's wife. You have no class."

"I took her to the boathouse, but Jack was already there with some young tomato." Sinatra thought back, replaying the scene in his mind. "It was Jack! Jack was the one who knocked the kid up."

"You can't lie your way out of this."

"Pat witnessed the whole thing. Just ask her."

"I'm not going to embarrass my sister by asking her to corroborate your disgusting lie."

Sinatra went on the offensive, backing Bobby against the cell door. "You fucking Kennedys are nothing but a bunch of hypocrites who hurt people and abuse power to get what you want, ignoring the truth to protect your own."

"I'm not buying it, Frank."

"And this is why you've hated me for so long? Because of something your brother did?"

Mortal enemies. Nose to nose.

"It was *you*. And you will rot in hell for what you did to that innocent girl. But before the devil gets his hands on you, you're going to rot in this jail cell until you agree to get me the evidence I need to convict Sam Giancana."

"Because of you, I can't get near Giancana."

"I suggest you figure out a way or else you'll be crushed by the entire weight of the Department of Justice and spend every day of the rest of your life in a cell like this, convicted of charges so heinous that even your most admiring fans will turn their backs on you. The name Frank Sinatra will be reduced to a punchline until the world eventually forgets all about you."

"Go fuck yourself, weasel."

"Sorry you feel that way, Frank. Have a pleasant evening."

CHAPTER 37

His eyes were wide open, but in the blackness, Sinatra could not see his hand in front of his face. Trying not to lose his marbles as, facing impossible odds, his brain processed the same thoughts over and over again. Freedom. Revenge. There could be no revenge without freedom. And no freedom unless he gave Bobby Kennedy what he wanted. His neck and back hurt from the hard cot. Did anyone even know he was missing? Probably not, as the swells at Jack Entratter's orphan shindig undoubtedly had spread gossip that he had flown to the moon with the go-go broad in the electric-pink minidress. The rancid slop he had been given for dinner was making him jones for the fusilli with garlic and anchovies at Villa d'Este. Freedom. Revenge. He had devised a course of action that would give him both, but it was extreme. A plan of last resort. He had one play to make first, but it was impossible from a jail cell.

Freedom. Freedom. Nothing without freedom. Freedom that could only be attained by lying to the weasel that he would get the evidence he wanted against Giancana. He couldn't, of course, because under the circumstances, he could not get near the mobster. Though he had witnessed Giancana murder George, blowing the whistle would not remove the Outfit target from his back. He had to stick to his plan and tell the weasel whatever he wanted to hear, because it would at least buy him a few days, the few days he needed to make his play. A nerve-racking few days as Giancana's words continually stabbed his brain: *Take a good look so you understand that seven days doesn't mean eight.*

Freedom.

The kink in his neck getting worse. Desperate for a cigarette. His guts churning. Would give his left nut for a plate of veal Milanese pounded paper-thin.

Light.

The silhouette of an enormous man filled the doorway, then quickly vanished into darkness as the steel door slammed shut behind him. Sinatra could sense the man feeling his way toward the cot, so he slid off toward the other side of the toilet, but that was as far as he could go. Hugged the wall until he felt the man draw near, then moved again. A game of cat and mouse where the mouse had no hope of escape. But that did not stop Sinatra from trying. He didn't care how big this bruiser was, he would knock him out if he could only see him. But in the blackness, all he could sense was his sour breath. Inches away. Freedom. Freedom. Nothing without freedom.

Sinatra fired a right hook in the direction of the smell that glanced off the man's chin, the miss giving away his position as the monster slammed him onto the cot. Yanked off his dungarees. Spread Sinatra's ass cheeks apart, and rammed his cock inside the smaller man. No lube, no spit, just a brutal anal assault that came hard and fast. Sinatra struggled, but it only made the pain worse as the monster jackhammered his ass until it was raw.

CHAPTER 38

Runny oatmeal meant it was morning.

Sinatra curled in a fetal position as his backside had been too brutalized for him to sit.

"Rough night, Frank?" Bobby Kennedy laughed as the cell door opened. "You look like hell."

Unwilling to show weakness, Sinatra sat on the edge of the bed, fidgeting as he tried to ease his pain. But he could not ease the fear of being squeezed by the attorney general of the United States on one side and the man who ordered murder with the same nonchalance as extra clams with his linguine on the other. He was fighting for his life. Thought about his kids, standing ovations, and Juliet Prowse's shaved pussy. The parties at Wonder Palms and wondered if he would ever see his home again.

No revenge without freedom.

"Sam Giancana has an illegal casino just outside of Chicago, a block down from the Villa Venice. He bragged that it made him more than five million dollars during the two weeks I was performing there."

"Can you tie him directly to the money?"

"If I tie Giancana to that money, I won't live five minutes."

"If you're scared, we can forget the whole thing and you can stay here. Three square meals a day. Plus, I heard you already made a friend."

No revenge without freedom.

"Let me out of here, and I'll get the evidence you need."

"You told me you couldn't get near Giancana."

"And you told me to figure out a way. So, I did."

Within minutes, military police escorted Frank Sinatra through a side gate of Nellis Air Force Base on the outer edge of North Las Vegas and released him back into the world wearing the baggy dungarees, a sweatshirt, and canvas slippers. No money or wallet, as he had been delivered to the lockup wearing only handcuffs. Didn't even have a dime to call for a ride as the sky darkened and it began to rain.

CHAPTER 39

Sinatra had not showered or shaved in almost a week. It was vital that he get to the Sands to clean up and collect his things, then disappear while he set his plan in motion. Outfit assassins were hunting him, and in a few days, Bobby Kennedy would figure out that he had been played. His balls in a vise, he held his thumb out to hitchhike. Only about fifteen miles away from the Strip, but it may as well have been a hundred, as even with the rain picking up, car after car passed without even slowing down. *And why would they?* Sinatra thought. He looked like a fucking tramp.

He pulled in his thumb and started walking. He moved past areas of open desert, soaking wet, and eventually, he came to a gas station and asked the attendant if he could use the phone.

"Phone booth outside."

"I don't have a dime."

"I'll give you change."

"I'm Frank Sinatra. I'd be grateful if you could help me out."

"Frank Sinatra would have money for the phone."

"I'll give you a hundred dollars when my ride gets here."

"Hit the bricks, you fucking bum," said the attendant, about to go out and service a beat-up station wagon that had pulled up to the gas pumps.

"Can I at least stay until the rain stops?"

"If you're still here when I get back, I'm calling the cops."

Sinatra ran out to the station wagon and told the woman behind the wheel that he would give her a hundred dollars for a ride to the Sands.

"Hop in, sugar."

The woman paid for the gas and tossed her change into the glove compartment, the pump jockey flipping Sinatra the finger as they drove off.

"Do you have a cigarette?"

"Sorry, sugar, I don't smoke."

"Hey, wait a minute," he said as he got his bearings. "Vegas is in the other direction."

"I know," she said as she continued down the road.

"I'll give you a grand. A thousand bucks to turn around and take me to the Sands."

"You don't have to pay me, sugar. I'll get you there." Her smile was missing a couple teeth. "But first I have to drop the groceries off at home."

The mention of food made him hungry. Looked in the back of the car and saw a large bag of Baby Ruth candy bars and a case of rum.

"You're having a party?"

"Why would you think that?" Her blond hair was tangled, and she was more than a little worse for wear, but it was easy to see that this woman had once been a looker. "Why don't you scoot a little closer, sugar, so we can get to know each other better?"

Nothing but desert in every direction, she turned off the highway onto an unpaved road that quickly diminished to a footpath. The rain was slowing as she drove for another mile or so, then wove the station wagon behind a large rock formation and stopped in front of what had probably once been a prospector's trailer. A couple weather-beaten lawn chairs sat out front.

Sinatra noticed the key still in the ignition as she got out to grab the groceries.

"I'll wait in the car."

"Don't be silly, sugar," she called back as she pulled open the tailgate. "It's lunchtime."

Sinatra looked at the key and thought better of it, then picked up the case of rum and followed her inside the smelly, dilapidated trailer.

"Dammit, Baby! You know better than to bring anybody here."

Sinatra thought he was seeing double as his eyes locked on two midgets with beards so long they almost dusted the floor. Each grabbed a bottle from the case and guzzled a long swallow.

"Who's this bum?"

"This is Sugar," Baby cooed as she wrapped her arms around Sinatra. "Can I keep him, Jeepers? Please, can I keep him?"

"Actually, my name is Frank. Frank Sinatra."

"And I'm the fucking Wizard of Oz."

"I *am* Frank Sinatra. And I'll give you a thousand dollars if you'll take me to the Sands. Or anywhere with a phone I can use."

"Baby, check his pockets."

She copped a feel, then turned the pockets of his filthy and still-damp dungarees inside out.

"Take me to a phone where I can call Jack Entratter at the Sands. He'll have someone bring you the money."

"A thousand bucks, you say?"

"However much it will take to get me to a phone."

"Tell me why Frank Sinatra would be out in the middle of the desert looking like a goddam hobo?"

"Get me to a phone, and I'll pay you whatever you want."

"Sing something."

"Why should I?"

"Because a man looking like a goddam hobo and offering big money when he ain't got one red cent in his pocket and claiming to be Frank Sinatra, had better figure out a way to convince me that he is Frank Sinatra." Jeepers took a slug of rum. "Elsewise his carcass is gonna get left for the buzzards."

"You better sing something, sugar."

"Please. Just get me to a phone."

Sinatra heard the crack of a shotgun and saw the midget aiming it at his head.

"What do you want to hear?"

"Anything, as long as it sounds like Frank Sinatra."

Baby swooned as he made with a few bars of "Come Fly With Me."

"Satisfied?"

"In the morning, I'll have Baby drive us to Moapa and call this fella at the Sands and find out just how much you're worth."

"Now. We have to call him right now."

"Got plans right now." The midgets chewed peyote and guzzled rum. "And you better hope this guy comes up with a lot more than a lousy thousand bucks or I'll blow your fucking head off."

"Go on outside and relax, sugar," Baby told Sinatra, thrilled that she had him all to herself until morning. "I'll fix us some lunch."

He tipped one of the weather-blistered chairs to dump off the rainwater, then sat down as the sun came out and bleached the sterile emptiness of rock and sand. Starving, at least he knew that whatever she was preparing for lunch would taste a lot better than the slop he had been fed in jail.

A few moments later, she came outside and unwrapped a Baby Ruth for each of them.

"A candy bar is lunch?"

"That's all I eat. Every meal."

So, they had candy bars for lunch. The first decent food Sinatra had eaten in days.

"Is that shotgun loaded?"

"You best believe it."

"How did you ever get involved with these guys?"

"We used to travel with a carnival. The Big Bill Burney outfit. Jeepers was a sharpshooter who used to shoot cigarettes out of my mouth blindfolded."

"What about the other one?"

"Creepers was a geek. Bit the heads off chickens for nickels and dimes the rubes threw at him. Then one day Jeepers robbed the carnival and killed Big Bill, and the three of us eventually ended up here, hijacking cars on the highway when we get low on grocery money."

"What happened to the old man who lived in this trailer?"

"How did you know he was an old man?"

"All prospectors are old men. Did Jeepers kill him?"

"Jeepers loves to kill people. Threw the leftover pieces of that old man down the mineshaft."

"Don't you get bored out here in the middle of nowhere?"

"I like it here. Most days we get high." She leaned close and rubbed his crotch. "But today you're gonna screw me till I can't stand up."

"Bucket!" Jeepers hollered from inside the trailer.

Baby planted a wet one on Sinatra's cheek. "Be right back, sugar."

She picked up a rusty bucket, then went inside where the midgets were whacked out of their skulls on the couch. Pushed their long beards to the side, and with a dick in each hand, peed them as if she were milking a cow.

Outside, Sinatra raced for the station wagon, got in, and reached to start it, but the key was missing.

A shotgun blast shattered the rear window.

"Get out of that car, sugar!" Baby yelled, aiming the shotgun at him.

Sinatra had no choice but to do as he was told.

"I'll blow your pretty head off if you even think about leaving without me."

"I thought you liked living out here."

"Do you have a piss bucket at your house?"

"No."

"Then I want to live with you instead."

"That sounds great," he smiled, turning on the charm.

"Don't say it if you don't mean it, sugar, or I swear to bloody Christ I'll blast your sweet ass to kingdom come."

"Believe me, Baby. I've never meant anything more in my life."

"Your house have a bathtub?"

"It has a swimming pool."

"Cross your heart?"

"Cross my heart. Now let's get the hell out of here." Sinatra won an Oscar but never had he delivered lines more convincingly. "Give me the key. I'll drive."

She lifted her dress, took the car key from her underwear, and handed it to him.

"Get your things," he told her.

"Don't have any things."

"Then go get the bag of Baby Ruths. We'll need them for dinner."

The second she stepped inside the trailer Sinatra fired up the station wagon. Tires kicking rock and sand, shotgun blasts falling short as he sped away toward the highway. He realized that showing his face at the Sands was a bad idea, given Giancana's deadline had passed, so he punched the gas toward Palm Springs. Probably also a bad idea but he needed to chance a quick stop at Wonder Palms for a hot bath to soak away a week of filth and degradation, then pack a bag and get on about the business of reclaiming his life.

CHAPTER 40

The loose coins in the glove compartment were just enough to top off the tank and power the station wagon through the back roads of the Mojave Desert to Amboy, Yucca Valley, and down the hill toward the evening lights of Palm Springs. With each passing mile, Sinatra became increasingly worried that a bullet would greet him the moment he opened his front door. As he rolled slowly down Wonder Palms Road, he looked for anything out of place. There were no strange cars, so he parked down the street and walked quickly to his house, found the spare key he kept hidden in the garden, and cautiously unlocked the door. He did not switch on any lights, leaving the house only partially lit, as it always was when he was away. There was no sign of an intruder, but an Outfit killer would hardly make himself known before getting the drop on his target.

George always had the kitchen stocked with Sinatra's favorites whenever he returned from a trip, but tonight, he found nothing but brown bananas and moldy cheese. Poured himself a drink and lit his first cigarette in a week. Tossed his prison clothes in the trash and went into the master bathroom where the shades were drawn and it was safe to turn on the light. Ran a bath, and as the tub was filling, he shaved and brushed his teeth twice. He was beginning to feel almost human as he soaked in the warm bath water, but had to be careful not stay in the house too long. He gave himself a thorough scrubbing, and as he rinsed the shampoo from his hair, he heard an odd hissing sound. Finished rinsing off, then was terrified by the ferocious roar of a ten-foot alligator that had him trapped in the bathtub.

The alligator lunged, clamping down its powerful jaws as Sinatra splashed out of the way. A hungry gator that might have been waiting in the house for a week, twisting and rolling before snapping its jaws as it came at him again. Sinatra couldn't get past and had nothing to hit it with, so he threw the bar of soap down the massive reptile's throat that distracted it but not enough for Sinatra to escape. He balled up a wet washcloth and threw it as hard as he could down its throat, causing the scaly beast to thrash wildly then again lunge at Sinatra, who squeezed the shampoo tube and shot a stream of Head & Shoulders into the alligator's eye, inducing a deafening roar. Then Sinatra shot shampoo into the other eye, causing the attacking beast to roll to one side while he scrambled the hell out of there and slammed the bathroom door shut.

It took quite a while for Sinatra to stop shaking as he sat on the edge of his bed and tried to decompress. Eventually able to stand, he put on a sport shirt and slacks, packed a small suitcase, and took some cash from his wall safe. He calmed himself with one more Jack on the rocks before walking down the street, firing up the station wagon with the shot-out rear window, and aiming it toward Los Angeles.

The most famous man in showbiz on the run like a cheap hood.

When he rolled into West Hollywood, he parked just below

Sunset Boulevard and walked to a Spanish Colonial apartment building around the corner. Made certain he was not seen as he entered and quietly knocked on the door at the end of the hall.

CHAPTER 41

Sinatra slipped past Angie, locked the door, and shut the curtains. His face was gaunt and the ever-present sparkle absent from his eyes.

She parked him on the sofa and handed him a drink.

"Have you eaten?"

"I had a Baby Ruth bar for lunch."

"I'll heat up some leftover casserole."

He emptied his glass, and she refilled it. Thinking how fortunate he was to have such a trusted friend.

The casserole was aces, and two more drinks had him struggling to stay awake.

"Take the bed, Frank. You need a good night's sleep."

In the past twenty-four hours Sinatra had been ass raped, blasted with buckshot and come within an eyelash of being eaten by an alligator. He would have no trouble sleeping.

"The sofa's fine," he said.

"I'll get some linens."

By the time she came back, he was conked out. She took off his shoes, slid a pillow under his head, and covered him with a blanket. Kissed him on the forehead and turned out the light.

After a solid ten hours in dreamland, Sinatra woke up refreshed.

"You're a fantastic cook," he complimented Angie between bites of a blueberry waffle and poached eggs.

"My grandmother taught me when I was a little girl back in North Dakota."

"Keep feeding me like this and I might marry you."

"Let's not ruin a good thing." She smiled. "What do you want for dinner? I'll go to the market."

"I'll give you a shopping list, but I'll make the dinner."

"And while I'm at the market, what will you be doing?"

"Meeting a guy at the beach. But right now, I have to call Mickey Rudin."

"Want privacy?"

"Not from you."

He picked up the phone and dialed Mickey's private number.

"Jesus, Frank," came the lawyer's gravelly voice on the other end of the line. "Where the hell have you been for the past week? Are you on a secure phone?"

"It's safe to talk."

"When I couldn't reach you, I was worried that the Outfit had. Nancy called to say that two goons crashed her honeymoon hotel looking for you."

"Is she okay?" he demanded, seething that Giancana had tried to get at him through his daughter.

"She's fine, Frank. Her new husband gave them a thrashing."

Frank began to see that maybe there was more to Tommy Sands than he had given him credit for.

"But she's scared because she can't find you. Nobody could find you."

Sinatra would call Nancy, but first he filled his attorney in on everything that had happened.

"Where are you now?"

"Someplace nobody in the world would think to look."

"I hate to say it, Frank, but I don't think we have any choice but to go to the police."

"Aren't you the one who said that the number-one rule when trying to keep the lid on something is to never involve the police? Especially now that I'm caught between Sam Giancana and the attorney general of the United States."

"Then what are we going to do?"

"You are going to call Dean and get a phone number."

"What phone number?"

"He'll know the one you mean. He won't want to give it to you but don't take no for an answer."

"I don't like the sound of this."

"Relax, Mickey. If I play my cards right, it will all be over this afternoon. The weasel, the Outfit, all of it." Then Sinatra's tone turned serious. "But just in case, get me that phone number."

"You're scaring me, Frank."

"And one more thing. Send somebody to Palm Springs to get that fucking alligator out of my bathroom."

Now that she knew the score, Angie was frightened.

"How bad is it, Frank?"

"I'll be better able to answer that question when I get back from the beach."

"Are you sure we're safe here?"

"I'm safe here. As for you, it all depends on how much you like my fusilli with garlic and anchovies."

CHAPTER 42

" How the hell did you get past the Secret Service?" Jack Kennedy yelled at Sinatra.

"This is *my* house," said his sister Pat, a cool breeze blowing in off the Pacific as she joined them on the deck of the Lawford beach house in Santa Monica. "And I want you to listen to what Frank has to say."

"Make it quick because Jackie is on her way back from shopping in Beverly Hills," said the president, wearing a sweater, khakis, and his usual tortoiseshell sunglasses as he sat on a deck chair smoking a cigar. Then looked at Pat. "What do you care about what he has to say anyway, and why the hell would you bring him here to say it? Especially when I'm gathering my thoughts before tonight's television address when I'm going to propose groundbreaking civil rights legislation."

"About fucking time you kept that promise," Sinatra said.

"Get to the point, Frank," the president pressed.

Frank's balls were in a vise, being squeezed by both the attorney general and the mob. It was his last chance to plead his case, but this time he was not banking on past friendships. This time he had an ace up his sleeve.

"Colleen Duffy."

"Who?"

"The teenage girl who worked for your family, got knocked up, then took a header off the Sagamore Bridge."

"I'm afraid I don't know who that is. So, if that's all you came here to say, you can turn around and leave."

"Knock it off, Jack," Pat snapped. "You know goddam well who she was."

"A high school kid," Sinatra said. "Starstruck and naive. And you took advantage of her."

"Bobby is convinced it was *you*."

"Probably because that's what you told him, and that's why he's had it in for me all these years. Come on, Jack. We all know it was you who screwed that innocent girl."

"She may have been a high school kid"—he laughed—"but that girl was anything but innocent."

"Then tell Bobby the truth."

"Why should I?"

"Because if you don't tell him to lay off me, and if you don't order him to stop all the organized crime surveillance *today*, I'll take the Colleen Duffy story to the newspapers."

Kennedy leaned on the railing and looked out over the ocean. He noticed that his cigar had gone out, then turned and looked confidently at Sinatra.

"You have no proof of anything."

"The newspapers might not see it that way. Especially when

they hear that Pat and I were at the boathouse that night and saw you screwing her."

"My popularity numbers have never been higher," Jack said. "The press will consider anything you say to be the resentment of a former friend and won't print a word."

"Are you willing to take that chance?" He looked at Pat, then back to Jack. "Are you willing to gamble your presidency that your sister will lie for you?"

"My sister will never betray me."

"He's right, Frank. I brought you here so you could plead your case because I think you're getting a raw deal, but I won't go against the family. Leave me out of it."

"Last chance, Jack," said Sinatra, still feeling he had the upper hand as he went toe-to-toe with the president of the United States. "Call off the organized crime surveillance today. No more bullshit about how it takes time. Get on the phone and call it off this minute or the newspapers will have the complete Colleen Duffy story in plenty of time for the morning editions."

"You're an immoral degenerate who took advantage of a high school girl in West Virginia," Jack said, "and now that you're caught again, you think you can shift the blame by attempting to blackmail the most popular president in recent memory. How do you think *that* will play out in the morning editions?"

"You don't scare me, Jack." Sinatra was not about to back down. "Call off Bobby or the Colleen Duffy story hits the front page."

"Have you forgotten I have that smut film you starred in?"

Pat glared at her brother, then went into the house.

"Look, Jack. You don't have to confess that you knocked the girl up, just tell Bobby it wasn't me and get him to back off. Because right now, he has me behind the eight ball where I'm either going to get two in the back of the head or get shanked in prison."

"You're being overly dramatic again, Frank."

"Dammit, Jack! If you don't stop the surveillance, Giancana is going to have me killed!"

"You need to leave."

"Are you so arrogant that you would allow me, an innocent man, to be murdered for something *you* did? Because unless you call off Bobby, I'm a dead man."

"You've always fancied yourself a gangster. Kill Giancana before he kills you." The president struck a match and relit his cigar. "Now get out before my wife comes back and finds you here."

As Sinatra turned to leave, Pat came back out and handed him the blackmail film.

"It was in the back of the bedroom closet where Peter stashes the pornographic magazines he thinks I don't know about."

"It doesn't change anything, Frank," Jack said as he sat back down on the deck chair and blew a smoke ring. "Because however this plays out, you're screwed."

CHAPTER 43

Frank's fusilli had been a hit, and the next night it was Angie's turn to cook as she did the prep work for chicken and dumplings.

"Didn't your grandmother teach you how to pound a veal chop or make carbonara?"

"For god sake, Frank. For once in your life, would it kill you to eat some good old-fashioned home cooking?"

"At my home that would be spaghetti and meatballs."

"Well, this is my home. You're going to eat whatever I put in front of you, and you're going to like it."

"Yes, ma'am," he said, winking at the woman who looked like a million in tight slacks and a cashmere sweater that fit like a second skin. But his mind was elsewhere.

When Kennedy threw him to the wolves, he knew there was only one way to stay alive. It was extreme. His last chance. He called the number Mickey Rudin had gotten for him, put the plan in motion, and in a few days, it would be time to call Giancana and settle the score once and for all. Nothing to do until then but stay out of sight and wait. He put a Tony Bennett record on the hi-fi, poured himself a drink, and caught up on all the smoking he had missed while locked in a jail cell.

Sinatra did eat what Angie put in front of him, and he did like it. Then he helped with the dishes and told her that tomorrow he would teach her the secret of his grandmother's red sauce.

For the next few days, Frank and Angie never left the apartment. They mostly played records and danced. She matched him drink for drink as they talked about everything and nothing. How she was up for the female lead in a remake of *The Killers* opposite Lee Marvin and Ronald Reagan. How he was thinking of recording an album with Count Basie and that he had added a new model train to his Wonder Palms funhouse. She made stuffed pork chops with gravy, and he spent an entire day preparing a traditional seven-course Italian feast. They watched popular television shows like *Ben Casey*, *Hawaiian Eye,* and *Alfred Hitchcock Presents*. It was like playing house without the complication of being married.

Finally, it was time. Everything was set. He called Giancana early in the day when Sinatra knew he would be home, both men aware that their words were being recorded.

"I'm surprised to hear from you, Frank."

"Meet me in Palm Springs tomorrow morning for coffee."

"That's a long way to go for coffee."

"It's good coffee, Sam. Be at my house at ten and don't be late."

The conversation was brief and cryptic, but there was no mistaking that someone was about to die.

It was Frank and Angie's last day together, and they spent it like every other day, except that when night fell, they ended up together in her bed. It was more than sex. It was magic.

Sinatra did not sleep, knowing what was ahead of him. The moment of truth. Before the sun rose, he took her lipstick and drew a heart on the bathroom mirror. Then he was gone.

CHAPTER 44

The flowers were dead, and Frank wondered where George had gotten the orange gladiolas that had always been in bloom around the house. Thought about all the things his friend had done that he had taken for granted, and how, in a matter of minutes, Frank would be face-to-face with the man who had murdered George.

The calm before the storm. He thought about his kids, about his first wife and how if she had been more like Angie, they might have made the marriage work. He thought about fame, fortune, and all the benefits of being the king of midnight. How he had one last chance to hang on to all of it. One last chance at freedom. It was all or nothing now, as he had already played his final card. There was no turning back. Someone was about to die. Nothing left to do but wait for the scene he had set in motion to play out.

George had once told Frank that the secret to his delicious coffee was to add a few drops of brandy to the filter, so he gave it a try. It wasn't as good as George's, but wasn't bad. He warmed up his new twenty-three-inch RCA just in time for the intro to *As the World Turns*, the most popular soap opera on television.

The doorbell rang.

The moment of truth was finally upon him.

Sam Giancana was flanked by two men in dark suits who pushed their way inside.

Frank was sickened at the sight of the man who had killed George but sucked it up, as it was what needed to be done.

Giancana scowled as he went into the living room and sat on the sofa.

"What the hell is this shit, Frank? You watching soap operas now?"

"All clear," the men in dark suits reported. "Nobody else in the house."

"I'll get you some coffee, Sam. I just made it."

"I don't want any goddam coffee. I want to know where you get the balls to send for me. Nobody *sends* for Sam Giancana."

"Lighten up, Sam. This is going to be a great day."

"You better tell me why you think so." Giancana gestured toward his men, who each put a gun to Sinatra's head. "And you better tell me quick."

One last chance at freedom, but he needed more time. No turning back. Someone was about to die, and it took every ounce of Sinatra's resolve to maintain his composure.

"You came all the way from Chicago. What's a few more minutes?"

"Why aren't you scared, Frank?"

"Watch the show, Sam."

A character named Nina told Grandpa that her son had invited his scheming ex-wife to Thanksgiving dinner. Sinatra was fixed on the soapy drama while Giancana grew rapidly impatient.

"Why are you stalling, Frank?" The mobster's eyes narrowed. "What the fuck are you up to?"

"Keep your shirt on. The good part is coming up."

"Fuck the goddam show!" Giancana screamed. "Tell me how you are going to make things right with the Outfit, and make it right *today*, or you won't live until the next commercial!"

Sinatra began to sweat.

It should have happened by now.

Two guns at his head.

He had taken an extreme chance.

His last chance.

Something had gone wrong.

Fire in Giancana's eyes.

Sinatra was out of time.

The wrong man about to die.

On the television, after Grandpa's initial shock, in the spirit of the holidays, he told Nina that it was nice of the boy to have invited his ex-wife to Thanksgiving dinner. Then all of a sudden, the soap opera characters were wiped from the screen, replaced by the words *CBS News Bulletin* and the voice of Walter Cronkite:

"In Dallas, Texas, three shots were fired at President Kennedy's motorcade in downtown Dallas. The first reports say that President Kennedy has been seriously wounded by this shooting... More details have just arrived. These details about the same as previously. President Kennedy shot today just as his motorcade left downtown Dallas. Mrs. Kennedy jumped up and grabbed Mr. Kennedy. She called 'Oh no' and the motorcade sped on. United Press says that the

wounds for President Kennedy perhaps could be fatal."

Giancana was stunned.

Sinatra sat quietly. Expressionless.

CBS returned to *As the World Turns*.

"I guess I misjudged you, Frank," Giancana said as he leaned back on the sofa and lit a cigar. He dismissed the gunmen to wait outside. "Maybe you *are* a gangster."

"I'm a performer," Sinatra told him as he made them each a drink, then settled into a chair opposite the sofa. "And after the hell I've been put through, that's all I ever want to be."

Walter Cronkite appeared again.

"From Dallas, Texas. The flash apparently official. President Kennedy died at 1:00 p.m. Central Standard Time."

"To you, Frank." Giancana raised his glass. A vicious gangster responsible for the murders of over two hundred men, in awe of the guts it had taken to kill the president. "What made you think you could pull it off? What gave you the idea?"

Sinatra was remarkably calm as he switched off the television.

"Bobby once told me that the only way to kill a snake is to cut off its head, though at the time he didn't realize he was talking about himself."

"Lyndon Johnson hates that prick Bobby almost as much as I do," Giancana said. "And it's a sure bet that one of the first things he'll do as the new president is fire that fucking snake, stopping the harassment so the Outfit can get back to doing business as usual. You're a hero, Frank."

"Take the target off my back."

"No more gunmen, and Marcello won't send any more

alligators," Giancana assured him. "And the way I see it, we owe you a big favor."

The man who had orchestrated the two most significant political events of the twentieth century saw it as confirmation that being Frank Sinatra was indeed better than being president. He had killed John Fitzgerald Kennedy in self-defense, taking back a life of which mere mortals dared not even dream. His conscience was clear as he adjusted the position of an oversized ashtray on the coffee table and lit a cigarette.

CHAPTER 45

Three months passed, and the country was moving forward. Sinatra played bartender at Wonder Palms for a few of his pals as they watched *The Ed Sullivan Show* because he had promised his daughter Tina that he would check out some new musical group from England that all the kids were losing their shit over. *Nice harmonies,* Frank thought. And though they showed the respect of wearing suits, would a trip to the barber shop have killed them? Popular today, but where would they be tomorrow? Certainly not drawing crowds of screaming teenagers like he had in the forties at the Paramount Theater on Broadway.

He never did cash in Sam Giancana's favor, as flying too close to the flame had taken the shine off the gangster lifestyle. Content just to be Frank Sinatra. Just? Movie star. Recording star. Knowing that Ed Sullivan's flavor of the week could never replace him as the biggest name in the music business. His life was a nonstop party, but he always found time to squeeze in some work. He had recorded that album with Count Basie, and a new Rat Pack movie called *Robin and the 7 Hoods* would be released in the summer.

And then like flipping a switch, a few friends watching television became a wingding as Jimmy Van Heusen walked through the door with three sexy women on each arm.

"Let's get this party started!"

EPILOGUE
1977

OVEREXPOSED

"Dammit," Jackie grumbled, seeing the camera as she and the McCaffreys approached the entrance of La Grenouille. The last place she would expected to encounter Ron Galella, a creepy tabloid photographer who had made a career out of violating her privacy.

Hank McCaffrey was a retired banker who liked martinis and baseball. His wife, Elisa, futzed in their garden and served him Yankee pot roast every Sunday. Hardly glamorous and a country mile from being famous, they had little in common with the former first lady who, two years earlier, had been widowed by Greek shipping billionaire Aristotle Onassis, except that they enjoyed each other's company. They had met at an auction of post-Colonial portraiture, became friends, and enjoyed dinner every month or so at this superb French restaurant on East Fifty-Second Street, the only spot in New York that made Jacqueline Kennedy Onassis feel as if she were in Paris.

Asparagus vichyssoise. Lobster medallions with avocado and grapefruit. Pan-seared foie gras. They sat at their usual table by the fireplace, where the McCaffreys talked about their recent river cruise along the Rhine and Jackie explained why she had abruptly quit her job as an editor at Viking Press, but it was obvious that Jackie was still bothered by the photographer. And before the lemon raspberry tartelette, Hank, who, as a banker, had always seen things in black and white, asked why she didn't have him arrested for invading her privacy.

"Because, believe it or not, what he's doing isn't illegal."

"Surely you can take him to court and get a restraining order."

"I have a restraining order that requires him to stay at least twenty-five feet away from me, but with a high-powered lens, it doesn't even slow him down. And to make matters worse, all the publicity he got from me taking him to court has created such a demand for his photos that he published a bestselling coffee-table book called *Jacqueline*."

Elisa didn't say much, but when she did, it was straight to the point. "What about a way to stop him that isn't quite so legal?"

"You want her to kill him?" Hank laughed.

"Why not?"

"Because, dear wife, the police would consider her the prime suspect."

"We could do it for her."

"I believe you're serious."

"Come on, Hank. When is the last time we did anything really exciting?"

"That's why I like the two of you," Jackie said. "Not only don't you want anything from me, but you would risk life in prison to help me."

They toasted their friendship.

"Maybe we could scare him off in some way that's a little less final," Hank suggested.

"Richard Burton knocked out one of his teeth and Elvis Presley's bodyguards slashed his tires. But nothing changed." Jackie went bottoms up with her wine. "And it's more than just annoying photos of me coming and going from restaurants and nightclubs. He pops out of doorways and from behind trash cans when my hair is windblown or I'm not looking my best. He once even chartered a helicopter and took pictures of me sunbathing topless on Ari's yacht."

"There must be something you can do," Elisa said.

"Unfortunately, it's a situation over which I have no control."

Or did she?

In the morning, Jackie made two phone calls. In the evening, she mixed cocktails in the living room of her penthouse overlooking Central Park. Always immaculately put-together even when dressed casually, she played social catch-up with longtime attorney Jay Bradshaw and *New York Times* publisher Arthur "Punch" Sulzberger.

"How are the kids?"

"Did you hear the latest about Diana Vreeland?"

"How are *your* kids?"

"Have you seen the revival of *Man of La Mancha*?"

Bradshaw, relaxed in a sweater and slacks, was always two steps ahead in any conversation, even if it was only small talk over cocktails. "What's on your mind, Jackie? Why did you ask to see us?"

Jackie had entrusted him with her legal affairs since that fateful day in Dallas and had known Punch Sulzberger, whose father had been a close friend of her father, since she was a little girl. They were honorable men she could trust with anything, experienced men who knew how to work both sides of the street.

"The restraining order against Galella isn't worth the paper it's printed on," Jackie complained. "So, how can I get that cockroach to leave me alone?"

"Legally, I'm afraid you have no other options."

"He's making my life a living hell. And not just me. That creep and the rest of the *National Enquirer* photographers are preying on a lot of celebrities, embarrassing them like *Confidential* and the other scandal sheets did in the fifties, costing them careers and marriages. They can't even skinny dip in their own backyard for fear that there is someone with a camera up a neighbor's tree."

Bradshaw attempted to ease her anxiety. "Nobody reads that trash, Jackie."

"Five and a half million people every week," countered Punch, proper as always in a blazer and tie, who monitored even the darkest corners of his industry. "And even if you are somehow able to get rid of Galella, other photographers will take his place—bolder and more invasive. This creep follows you down the street, but the next guy might have eyes in your bedroom."

"I can't go on living this way." Jackie was angry. She gulped the rest of her Negroni and mixed another. "I have to do something."

Bradshaw was again thinking ahead. "The only way to stop Galella and others like him is to eliminate the marketplace. If there is no one to buy the photos, they will stop taking the photos."

"You can't possibly be suggesting that Jackie buy the *National Enquirer*," Punch said.

"Attorney-client privilege does not apply when a third party is present, so I advise, for Jackie's sake, that you go into the kitchen and make a sandwich."

"He stays," Jackie said.

"As you wish. But I will give him a last chance to reconsider risking his own reputation as well as that of his newspaper."

"The public relies on the *New York Times* to deliver the news, the real news, in a fair and unbiased manner," Punch declared. "And to preserve the dignity of my newspaper as well as that of the publishing profession, I will do whatever is in my power to help Jackie bring this scum to his knees so that she can regain her privacy."

"Get off your soapbox, Punch," Bradshaw said. "We get the point."

"I meant every word, counselor. Now, stop beating around the bush and tell us your goddam plan."

"I suggest that we blackmail the publisher of the *National Enquirer*," Bradshaw told them. "Tell us everything you know about him."

"Generoso Pope Jr. is an embarrassment to the industry, who defends his practice of celebrity stalking by calling it personality journalism," Punch told them. "And I have it on good authority that he has issued a standing order that there is to be a cover story or cover line on Jackie in every issue."

Jackie slammed down her glass as Punch continued.

"His father was publisher of the Italian language newspaper *Il Progresso*. Junior learned the ins and outs of the business there, then bought the *New York Enquirer* and transformed it into the *National Enquirer*, a supermarket tabloid where the cover always touted things like phony cancer cures and UFO sightings, gory murder stories and morgue photos. The public ate it up and wanted more, so he set his sights on America's most glamorous mystery: Jackie. And he does not hide the fact that he pays top dollar for stories. No matter what the cost if it's juicy enough."

"What about his personal life?" Bradshaw wanted to know.

"I understand that he lives in Lantana, Florida," Punch said. "A small beach town near Boca Raton where his business is located."

"What are his vices?" Bradshaw pressed. "What dirty deals has he made?"

"Word is that he bought the *New York Enquirer* with money borrowed from mob boss Frank Costello."

"It's enough to start with," Bradshaw said. "We will hire a detective to go through Pope's trash for personal letters, receipts, empty prescription bottles, and anything that might be incriminating. Follow him and take compromising photos of him screwing his secretary or whatever it is he's hiding. Because it has been my professional experience that men like Pope are always hiding something."

"And we use the evidence to blackmail him into leaving me alone?" Jackie asked.

"That's the idea," her lawyer told her.

"But what if he doesn't go for it?"

Punch Sulzberger was also one to think ahead. "Then we go public with whatever dirt the detective digs up by printing a phony tabloid front page with scandalous pictures of Pope under a sensational headline and wrap it around old tabloid filler. Place it on newsstands and in supermarkets in select major cities."

"You can make that happen?" Jackie smiled at the irony of beating Pope at his own game.

"I know printers and news agents all over the country who will do anything, and keep their mouth shut, for the right price," Punch said.

"And if he still doesn't agree to leave me alone?"

"Then we air his dirty laundry with another phony edition the following week, and every week until he does agree."

The next day, Jay Bradshaw set the plan in motion, engaging a detective who would cross any line necessary to achieve the desired result, who checked into a motel in Lantana, Florida, and immediately went about the business of digging up dirt on Generoso Pope.

Pope went to work every morning at the *National Enquirer* building, then at night returned home to his wife and kids. But not every night. At least once a week he cruised the rougher gay bars in Miami, doing copious amounts of bathroom cocaine before taking muscular men with hairy chests to seedy motels where there was no chance of him being recognized. But that was his only precaution, which allowed the New York detective to take several rolls of incriminating photographs, even through the window of his room.

Jackie found herself with a lot of free time since quitting her job at Viking, spending afternoons lunching with friends or hiding behind oversized sunglasses as she caught up on her reading in Central Park. The glamorous Jackie O, today comfortable in jeans and a sweater, noticed a woman on the bench across from her holding a French magazine, who after a few minutes got up and walked toward her.

"Bonjour, Jacqueline."

Jackie took off her sunglasses, eyes sparkling as she faced the woman she had known so intimately almost three decades ago while studying art history in Paris. The woman who pronounced her name Jacquel*een*, and now, just as then, hearing her say it gave her a chill.

"You never answered my letters," Jackie said.

"I wrote you faithfully." Caroline sat beside her on the bench.

Long raven hair with a bit of natural curl, her beauty touched little by time.

"My mother must have intercepted them."

"She knew about us?"

"The way my face lit up when I spoke about you, she suspected. Gave me a long lecture about how even a hint of scandal would ruin any chance of me marrying well."

"You married very well."

"I was blessed with two beautiful children."

"Your daughter…"

"Yes," Jackie smiled. "I named her after you."

Caroline wiped a tear from her eye.

"But my marriage to Jack was cursed from the start by his constant infidelity. Then when he died, the entire world came crashing down on top of me. I often fantasized about disappearing somewhere with you and the children." Jackie touched her hand. "Did you marry?"

Caroline told her of an abusive ex-husband and a series of dead-end jobs.

"When my spirits were low, I would often go to Café Louchard and sit for hours in the back booth where we first kissed." She smiled at the woman she had loved all those years ago. "Always feeling better walking out than when I had walked in."

They crossed Fifth Avenue to Jackie's apartment, where they sipped champagne and reminisced about the day the free-spirited Caroline first met the very proper Jacqueline Bouvier at the English-language bookstore Shakespeare and Company. How opposites attracted and they became inseparable.

A kiss took them back to Café Louchard. Another led to Jackie's bedroom.

In the morning, Jackie made mushroom omelets with brie and chives—Caroline's favorite. They talked, and they laughed. Then over coffee in the living room, Caroline showed Jackie two black-and-white photographs from their time together in Paris: one with them kissing, and the other of Jackie naked on Caroline's bed.

Jackie smiled as she remembered.

"I told you that mine has so far not been a successful life, and opportunities are few for a woman my age."

"Tell me how I can help you, Caroline. Anything."

"I would never impose upon you, Jacqueline. But I must tell you that the man who publishes the *National Enquirer* has offered me a lot of money for these photographs."

"Caroline, you can't!"

"I will not, my love. I would never betray you like that, but the fact remains that I need to support myself."

Her kids. Her reputation. Jackie knew that if Generoso Pope got his hands on those photographs, it would mean the end of life as she knew it.

"How much did he offer you? I'll double it."

"One hundred thousand dollars."

Jackie told Caroline that she would arrange to get her the money, then paused a moment and looked oddly at her.

"How did he know you had these photographs?"

Caroline was caught off guard by the question.

Jackie's eyes narrowed on her.

"It's because you went to Pope first. These are copies because he already paid you for the originals."

"You must understand my position, Jacqueline."

"What I understand is that the woman I held dear in my heart for almost thirty years came here to betray me and to steal from me."

Jackie pushed Caroline out the door and slammed it behind her, then called the doorman to have her escorted from the building.

Late that afternoon, Jay Bradshaw and Punch Sulzberger arrived at her apartment to make final preparations before pulling the blackmail trigger on Generoso Pope.

Bradshaw took the lead.

"Our detective is ready to go back to Florida, where he will offer to trade Pope a few incriminating photos in exchange for respecting Jackie's privacy."

"Pope won't be there," Jackie told him. "He's on his way to New York."

"Then we'll have the detective approach him here."

Punch opened his briefcase and handed them each a mock-up of the fake tabloid cover he had put together featuring pictures of Pope snorting cocaine with two naked men in a cheap motel room below a headline that screamed:

DOPE FIEND PUBLISHER, NATIONAL ENQUIRER BOSS CAUGHT IN DRUG DEN

"If he refuses to play ball, the presses will roll out fifty thousand copies that will be strategically placed on newsstands and in supermarkets across the country. And if he still refuses, we distribute this one the following week."

GENEROSO POPE IN GAY SEX ROMP

"We can't blackmail Pope," Jackie told him.

"Why not? We have him right where we want him."

"Pope has two very compromising photos of me, photos that would destroy the lives of myself and my children. So, I called and arranged to meet him for their return in exchange for photos of him on a cocaine binge with naked men."

"You can't confront him like that, Jackie. The man has mob ties. He's dangerous."

"I don't care. I'm going to do what needs to be done."

"What if *he* doesn't care?" Bradshaw asked. "Some powerful men don't mind public embarrassment if there is a lot of money to be made."

"Being outed might be embarrassing," Jackie said. "But cocaine is illegal."

"I doubt those pictures would be admissible in court."

"But they would in divorce court. He would stand to lose his kids and half of everything he has, including his precious scandal sheet."

The following morning Jackie and Pope agreed to an exchange of photographs.

Jackie and Pope each lied that there were no copies, each secure in the knowledge that the other had too much to lose to risk a double cross.

The photos of her and Caroline safely in her purse and her reputation intact, Jackie enjoyed a feeling of victory as she walked through the park on her way home. A feeling that evaporated the moment she realized that after everything that happened, nothing had changed, leaving her right back where she started. Fair game for any sleazeball with a camera.

She sat on a bench and through oversized sunglasses watched the world pass by. Joggers and dog walkers. Nannies pushing strollers. Young lovers holding hands, making her think about that first kiss in the back booth of Café Louchard.

LET'S GET THIS PARTY STARTED

"Times have changed since the corruption of 1960," Ronald Reagan told Sinatra as they chatted in the living room at Wonder Palms. "The Kennedys are dead, Giancana is dead, and votes are now counted fair and square."

"I appreciate you making the drive down from the ranch," Frank said, looking casually sharp in an orange cardigan, though advancing years necessitated that he wear a toupee in order to maintain his appearance. "But I'm afraid you wasted the trip."

"All I'm asking is that you try to flip some of those bleeding-heart Hollywood liberals. Make them realize, like you did, that supporting Republicans, especially *this* Republican, is supporting progress for everyone."

"You shouldn't have any trouble beating Carter. Besides, that election isn't for another three years."

"Even though it was Nixon's mess, the party is still trying to get out from under the cloud of Watergate, and that's how that damn peanut farmer got elected in the first place. I need to start my campaign now and start it strong, and that includes having you provide the star power."

"I was told once that I'm an immoral degenerate whose name could sink a campaign."

"Are you kidding?" Reagan laughed, looking fit in a Western shirt and slacks. "Last year half the country watched you reunite Dean Martin and Jerry Lewis on the Muscular Dystrophy Telethon. America loves you, Frank."

"And so do I," smiled Frank's wife Barbara, a stylish middle-aged blonde, as she brought him a fresh drink and refilled Reagan's favorite California burgundy. "What are you boys talking so seriously about?"

"Ronnie wants me to help with his presidential campaign."

"Good luck with that," Barbara laughed. Then went into the dining room to join Nancy Reagan setting the table for neighbors and friends about to stop by for a potluck supper.

Reagan kept pushing, finally telling Frank that if he publicly supported his candidacy, he would appoint him ambassador to Italy.

"There was a time when I might have jumped at that offer, but right now, I have the perfect life. I play Vegas and a few dates on the road. I hang out with pals at the local spots, then come home to Barbara. It's all I need, and it's all I want." They had been married over a year, but the newlywed sparkle was still in Frank's eyes as he looked at his wife in the dining room. "You know, Ronnie, she and I don't always see eye to eye, but that woman saved my life by giving me a reason to come home. I don't need to stay out all night or throw wild parties anymore."

"Wonder Palms parties are legendary, and word is that Jimmy Van Heusen never walks into this house unless he has three sexy women on each arm."

"Times change. People change."

"Not everyone."

"Everyone, Ronnie. Most people downshift when they get older. You're different because ambition drives you to punch the gas, but it's still change."

Reagan watched Frank light a cigarette, then lean back on the sofa, knowing that no matter in what capacity, he would be an asset to his candidacy.

"How about helping me wrangle some major donations? Maybe host a private party with some of Jimmy's special talent."

"Sorry, Ronnie. I'm just not interested. Besides, rich men have no problem getting hot young stuff on their own."

"But with you involved, it adds glitz and glamour their money can't buy. Maybe Jimmy would be interested. Will you at least ask him?"

"Ask him yourself. He'll be here in a few minutes."

Frank enjoyed playing host as guests began to arrive, making drinks and spinning records. The men lied about golf scores and kibitzed about whether or not the Dodgers had a chance against the Yankees in the World Series, while their wives arranged a buffet of the potluck dishes they had brought.

Reagan tried one last time to convince Frank to help elect another president.

"I appreciate the offer, Ronnie, and I'm flattered you think I could help your campaign. But I learned a long time ago that being Frank Sinatra is a lot better than anything else in the world, and I want to enjoy every minute of it." He looked adoringly across the room at his wife. "Now more than ever."

"Let's get this party started!" Jimmy Van Heusen called out.

"See, Frank, not everyone has changed," Reagan said with a confident laugh. Then his expression fell as he saw Jimmy carrying a casserole dish as he walked through the door with his wife.

ACKNOWLEDGEMENTS

Special thanks to my lovely wife Katie, and to Allan Carter and Scott Dickensheets for helping make this book a reality. To the wonderful Carolyn Uber for making all my books a reality. To Tara McCrillis and everyone at IDW. Dirku, Arpee, and Hoss. Ally Carter, Steve Fahlsing, and Jenn O. Cide. Amy and Lance. Chris Andrasfay, Gunther, Treehouse, Josh Petty, and Dr. Dick. Ginger Bruner and Dayvid Figler. The Yorkshire Mob. Jay and Star. The Fuck Dots. Ace Hogenson and Davey Klubs. And especially to my first editor, Geoff Schumacher, for pushing me to write another Las Vegas book. Thank you, Geoff. I'm very grateful you did.

ABOUT THE AUTHOR

P Moss is an author whose twisted crime novels seamlessly blur the line between fact and fiction. A film noir and pulp fiction enthusiast, he owns bars in Las Vegas and New York City, and is an avid supporter of Scunthorpe United F.C. Learn more at PMoss.com.